W9-AIB-055

Historical Fiction Adventures

Captain Hannah Pritchard

The Hunt for Pirate Gold

Bonnie Pryor

Enslow Publishers, Inc.
40 Industrial Road
Box 398
Berkeley Heights, NJ 07922
USA

http://www.enslow.com

For my daughter Jenny.
Without her help I could not have finished this book.

Library of Congress Cataloging-in-Publication Data

Pryor, Bonnie.
Captain Hannah Pritchard : the hunt for pirate gold / Bonnie Pryor.
p. cm. — (Historical fiction adventures (HFA))
Summary: Still disguised as a boy, now-seventeen-year-old Hannah Pritchard and her crew aboard the ship Hannah carry out missions for the Continental navy while searching for lost pirate treasure and trying to evade an evil pirate captain.
Includes bibliographical references.
ISBN 978-0-7660-3817-2
[1. Sea stories. 2. Adventure and adventurers—Fiction. 3. Buried treasure—Fiction. 4. Sex role—Fiction. 5. Pirates—Fiction. 6. United States—History—Revolution, 1775-1783—Fiction.] I. Title. II. Title: Hunt for pirate gold.
PZ7.P94965Cap 2011
[Fic]—dc22 2010050343

Paperback ISBN 978-1-59845-283-9

Printed in the United States of America
062011 Lake Book Manufacturing, Inc., Melrose Park, IL
10 9 8 7 6 5 4 3 2 1

Illustration Credits: Library of Congress, p. 154; National Archives and Records Administration, pp. 155, 156; Original Painting by © Corey Wolfe, p. 1; © 2011 Photos .com, a division of Getty Images, p. 157.

Cover Illustration: Original Painting by © Corey Wolfe.

Contents

The Story So Far . . .

The following is a brief account of the adventures Hannah Pritchard had before the tale you are about to read. Should you like to know in detail about all the close calls Hannah had and the battles she fought, check out **Hannah Pritchard: Pirate of the Revolution** and **Pirate Hannah Pritchard: Captured!** by Bonnie Pryor.

The year is 1777 and the American colonies are fighting for independence from Britain. When a combined force of British, Tories, and Iroquois attacks Hannah Pritchard's family farm, she manages to escape. But the rest of her family is killed in the massacre. Vowing revenge, she makes her way to Portsmouth, New Hampshire, where, disguised as a boy, she signs on as a cabin boy on the American privateer ship the *Sea Hawk*. After capturing a British ship, part of the crew is sent back to Portsmouth with the prize ship and part of the crew remains with the *Sea Hawk*, including Hannah.

The *Sea Hawk* is then attacked and sunk by the British. However, Hannah and her friends—Dobbs, the cook, and Daniel—escape with a chest of Spanish doubloons. They bury the treasure on an island. But the following morning, the British capture them. They are taken to New York and sentenced to the terrible prison ships in the East River. After enduring months of disease, starvation, and hardships, they manage to escape. They capture another British ship with the help of some new friends and begin to sail back to Portsmouth.

Now, in 1780, Hannah and her friends need to find the buried treasure. But first they must complete some important missions for the Continental navy. How will they find the treasure? What evils will they encounter? Continue reading to explore Hannah's next great adventure.

chapter one

The Sea Serpent

It was the darkest night Hannah had ever seen. Thick clouds obscured every hint of moonlight. Holding onto a lantern in one hand and a mug of tea in the other, she carefully threaded her way around coils of ropes to the captain's quarters. Sniffing appreciatively, she breathed in the smell of newly sawed wood and clean, billowing sails. The *Hannah*, the ship named after her, was a trim three-masted schooner. They had captured it right under the nose of the British captain, who had come to take possession of it. It had been built to bring supplies from the West Indies to the British troops stationed in the New York area, and no expense had been spared.

Just off the quarterdeck were three generously sized officers' rooms. The captain's quarters were truly luxurious, with a mahogany desk and plump stuffed chairs. The best thing, however, was the galley. It was larger than most with a large oak table for extra working space. The stove was new, and, best of all, it had a brick bake oven on one side. As soon as they reach port, Hannah thought, she would purchase flour to make the crew some real biscuits. The ship's biscuits were so hard that even after soaking them in coffee or grog, they could almost break a sailor's teeth.

She reached the stairs to the quarterdeck, but out of the darkness a voice called out from the rail.

"Jack? Is that you?"

Hannah recognized the voice of Thomas, one of the new sailors from New York. Most of the crew members called Hannah by the name Jack. Only three people knew that she was actually a girl disguised as a boy. Now that she was nearly seventeen, it was increasingly difficult to maintain her disguise as a boy.

"Yes," she answered, keeping her voice low. "I am taking tea to the captain's quarters."

"Come over here and look out over the rail for a minute," Thomas said, as he pointed to the sea.

Hannah peered carefully. "I don't see anything," she said after a minute.

"Keep looking," Thomas insisted. "I'm sure I saw something."

She stared out at the rolling black waves. "I don't see anything Thomas. What do you think you saw?"

Thomas shook his head. "I thought I saw something moving—something big!"

"Maybe a whale?" Hannah suggested.

"Maybe," Thomas said doubtfully. He pointed to the tea. "You had better get that over to Captain Dobbs before it gets cold."

Hannah continued on her way, balancing the tea. She tapped at the captain's door. "I brought you some tea," she said when Dobbs opened the door. He looked tired.

"Thanks," he said, taking the cup. Before he could even set the cup on his desk, Thomas came running across the quarterdeck.

"Captain Dobbs! Captain Dobbs!" Thomas hollered excitedly. "There is something out there. Jack didn't see anything, but I just saw it again. I think it is a sea serpent. I saw a head, huge black wings, and a long black body."

Dobbs looked pale as he grabbed the looking glass. Everyone had heard rumors of sea serpents, but no one that Hannah knew had ever seen one. They stared for several minutes. However, there did not seem to be anything but the sea and the sky, as black as ink.

"I saw something," Thomas pleaded.

Dobbs patted his shoulder. "Maybe it is gone now," he said reassuringly. Hannah listened intently over the slap of the ocean waves. She thought she heard another sound. She listened again. There was the faint sound of a wooden ship, the creak of rigging, and the gentle flap of a sail caught in the wind.

"I think it's a ship," she said.

But her words were lost in a chorus of fearful gasps and moans from the crew gathered at the rail. Across the water, a terrible sight rose to stare at them, glowing eyes burning like fire cast an evil spell. From the light of its eyes, they could see a long snout, gleaming sharp teeth, and dark wings unfolded in the wind.

"We be doomed!" Thomas shouted.

Hannah shuddered. What if the sea monster capsized the ship and ate them one by one? Would a sea monster swallow you whole, she wondered. She thought about being in the monster's stomach. Would you slowly dissolve as the monster digested you? Or would the monster chew you up before swallowing? She shuddered again at the thought of being chewed up, her bones cracking between the monster's teeth. The vision only lasted a few seconds, and then the beast turned away. Daniel, one of Hannah's best friends, had come onto the deck to see what the commotion was, and he reached for Hannah's hand in the dark and squeezed it.

"Are you all right?" Daniel asked her with genuine concern in his voice.

"Listen," Hannah said tensely. Again, she heard the same sounds she had heard before the beast showed its face. "I think that there's a ship out there."

"Quiet!" Dobbs ordered. Everyone held their breath, and there was a thick silence. However, there were no more sounds. If it had been a ship, they could not hear it anymore.

"What if the monster is under the water?" Thomas said in a hushed voice. "It could come up and capsize us."

"I have been at sea for thirty years," Dobbs said evenly. "And I have never seen or heard of a real sea monster."

"That doesn't mean that there isn't such a thing," said James, one of the seamen.

"I think that it's a ship," Hannah said. "I don't know how or why it made that horrible face, but I am sure I heard the sounds of a wooden ship."

They listened intently, but the night was silent.

"Whatever it was, it seems to be gone now," Dobbs said. "Let's get back to work."

They all went back to work, but everyone was nervous and jumpy. After an hour went by, Hannah began to relax. With all the excitement, she had missed most of her time to sleep. She would have to cook breakfast soon, and it was too late to get any sleep. She leaned on the rail staring out at the dark sea and thought about how glad she would be to see the first light of day.

Daniel came up and stood beside her. "I think it's out there again," Hannah told him quietly. Daniel nodded in agreement.

"This time I hear it, too. It's like they are playing cat and mouse with us," Daniel said.

"Who are 'they'?" Hannah mused. "The British are so organized and orderly. I can't imagine them with a ship that looks like a serpent."

"Perhaps they are real pirates," Daniel said. Hannah climbed the quarterdeck and went down the hall to the captain's quarters.

"Captain Dobbs," she called out softly. "I am sorry to disturb you, but I think they are out there again."

Dobbs hurried out and looked, but before he could raise his looking glass to his eye, there was a flash of light and a very loud boom. A cannonball soared overhead and narrowly missed the ship.

Instantly, Dobbs called down to James, who was at the wheel. "Hard right!" he shouted. The ship lurched, obeying James's maneuvers. But there was another flash, and a cannonball sailed over the rail of the main deck before falling harmlessly into the sea.

Hannah gasped, "Where are they?"

From the darkness came a voice, "Ahoy there! My guns are ready and aimed right at you. You have five minutes to launch your ship's boats with your crew, or we will sink your ship."

"We would never survive in the open sea," Dobbs shouted back to the voice.

"That is your problem," the voice answered. "You now have four minutes."

Several of the crew had run up from below. "Should we ready a gun?" one of them asked.

Dobbs shook his head. "There are only eight of us. There is no way to keep even one gun going."

"Wait!" Hannah shouted, almost forgetting to lower her voice like a boy. "Are you British?"

"No!" the voice thundered. "I am Captain Samuel Cutter of the American ship the *Sea Serpent*."

At this, Thomas looked at Hannah. Despite their danger, he appeared relieved that he had not been made the fool.

"We are not British either. We are the American ship *Hannah* headed for dock at Portsmouth," Dobbs called back to Captain Cutter.

"If you are not British, why are you flying an English flag?" the captain shouted back.

"We are American privateers, and we just captured this ship from the British."

"Captain, hold your lantern up so that I can see you," Captain Cutter asked after a brief silence.

Dobbs did as he was told, and there was a chuckle from across the water.

"I can tell that you are American. No British captain would ever be caught dead in ragged clothes like that. I recommend that you take down that English flag."

"I plan to do so once I reach Portsmouth," Dobbs replied.

"Portsmouth is where I am headed as well. I'll see you there." And with that, the voice of Captain Samuel Cutter disappeared into the darkness.

chapter two

Portsmouth

The next morning, as they approached Portsmouth, Daniel worked high above the deck furling the sail on the mizzenmast. Hannah kicked off her boots and nimbly scampered up the main mast to the topsail. As she passed Daniel, he grinned. Hannah knew that he remembered the first time she had climbed the ropes and how frightened she had been. The ship was sailing with an inexperienced crew. Only one of them had served on a ship before. Mostly, they were farm boys or shipbuilders' sons. Several had been violently seasick the whole trip. Normally, Hannah would not have been required to climb the ropes. However, because they were so shorthanded, she and Daniel had done most of the climbing.

Most sailors climbed the ropes in their bare feet because a shoe could slip, and a fall to the deck from that height would result in terrible injuries or even death. On this morning, in late winter 1780, the ropes were covered with ice, and Hannah's feet were soon numb. Tiny pricks of pain shot through her toes. Trying to ignore the pain, she unlatched the topsail, wrapped it around a bar, and tied it securely. From this height, she could see the outline of the town. It was enveloped in a shroud of fog, but the day was dawning bright and clear. A perfect blue sky and a bright sun would soon burn off the last tendrils of fog.

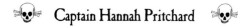

When she had climbed down, one of the crew tossed Hannah a pair of warm wool socks.

"Thanks, John," Hannah said gratefully. "The first thing I want to do when we get to port is buy new socks and boots."

Hannah, Daniel, and Dobbs, who was acting as captain, had escaped from a prison ship with no more than the ragged clothes on their backs. After their escape, they had managed to capture this brand-new British ship loaded with provisions from right under the British patrol's nose. They changed the ship's name from the *Elizabeth* (named after a British queen) to the *Hannah*.

Hannah hurried to the galley to make sure everything was tidy and put away carefully. By the time she went back up to the main deck, she saw Daniel looking out over the rail.

"We made it, Hannah," Daniel said softly, so no one could hear him.

The fog had lifted and she could see the wharf and Queen Street winding away. She could see the red roof of the Red

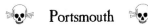

Rooster Inn. The Red Rooster had become her home after the British, Tories, and Iroquois had murdered her family. Madeline and Lottie, the owners of the Red Rooster, had not only given her a job but also love and support. She thought fondly of her days with the two ladies. The need for revenge for her parents' and brother's death was too great, however, and she had joined the crew of a ship called the *Sea Hawk*. She wanted to fight the British.

Now, the *Sea Hawk* had been sunk, and Captain Nelson had gone down with his ship. With Captain Nelson's help, Hannah, Daniel, and Dobbs had managed to save a huge chest of Spanish doubloons. They buried it somewhere on an island in the Outer Banks near the Carolinas. But just after burying the treasure, they were captured by British soldiers. They had spent months aboard a terrible prison ship starving and sick before escaping.

"Look at that," Daniel exclaimed. He pointed to a large ship. It was completely black with a yellow stripe around the rail. A ferocious serpent's head was fastened to the bow so that the ship looked like a giant sea serpent. The sails were furled, but they could see the sails were black.

"That must have been the ship that fired on us last night," Hannah said. "No wonder Thomas thought he saw a sea serpent."

The ship was heavily armed. Hannah could see two swivel guns at the bow. Hannah heard raucous voices from the crew members of the black ship as they disembarked.

"Look," she said, nudging Daniel. All of the men were dressed in black vests, shirts, and boots. It was impossible to discern their hair color because each of them wore black knitted caps. Jostling each other boisterously, they headed for the rough part of town, where there were rundown taverns, brothels, and cheap inns.

Daniel still stared at the ship. "Now that looks like a fighting ship," Daniel said with a hint of envy. But there was no time to admire the ship. The *Hannah* had docked and the work of selling the goods would soon begin.

Dobbs took Hannah aside. "I have to find the judge to declare that the goods in the hold are eligible to be sold."

Dobbs returned in a few hours with an agent of the court. This agent would supervise the sale and ensure that the government received 10 percent of the proceeds.

The *Hannah* was quickly unloaded, crates opened to display their contents. Merchants came with wagons to bid on goods. Under the watchful eye of the court agent, Daniel, who was good with sums, wrote down the amounts in neat columns as each crate was sold.

Dobbs spoke with the wharfmaster. Before the *Sea Hawk* had been sunk, it had captured another British ship without a fight. Mr. Gaines, the *Sea Hawk*'s first mate, had taken part of the crew to sail the ship back to their home dock at Portsmouth. But that had been more than two years earlier. Dobbs returned after a few minutes with news that Mr. Gaines was given a commission in the Continental navy. Mr. Gaines did not know how long it would be before he returned, so he left the money from the sale of the captured ship on account with the wharfmaster.

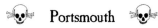

Dobbs handed Hannah and Daniel some coins. "Buy yourselves some clothes and shoes. I will join you later at the Red Rooster Inn."

Hannah clutched the money, and they began to peer into shops. "I'm anxious to see Madeline and Lottie, but I am so sick of wearing these awful ragged clothes. We will have to stop and get something new to wear. We can change at the inn and maybe even get a bath."

Near the wharf, they found a store displaying sailor's clothing. The clerk frowned when he saw them, but he became friendlier when he saw they had money. Hannah selected loose-fitting trousers, a long shirt, and a vest. The clerk wrapped their purchases in brown paper and tied it with string.

The proprietor of the cobbler store was a kindly old man with a twinkle in his eyes. He carefully measured their feet. "Come back in the morning young sirs. Your feet will think they have died and gone to heaven. Most of my profession makes both shoes to fit one pattern. I make a pattern for each foot."

At last, they headed for the inn. "I will be so happy to see Madeline and Lottie. I wonder if they will recognize me," Hannah said. "I hope that they are not angry that I left without telling them."

She pushed open the door. It was midmorning and only a few customers sat in the dining room. Through the open kitchen door, she could see Madeline taking bread from the oven. Madeline stared at her for a moment and then shrieked with joy, nearly dropping the loaves that she had in her hands. Her brown skin gleamed with sweat from the hot ovens.

"Hannah, child, is that really you?" She rushed over and gave Hannah a fierce hug. "We just received your letter last week. Did they let you go?"

"I wrote that letter months ago. We escaped!" Hannah said. "You must call me Jack. Everyone except for my friends Daniel and Dobbs think that I am a boy. Where is Lottie?"

"She is at the bank trying to borrow money. We were going to see if we could buy your freedom."

Lottie burst through the door just then. "I was at the bank when I happened to look out the window. I was sure it was you!"

She hugged Hannah. They sat together at one of the tables. Hannah introduced Daniel, and they told Madeline and Lottie the story of their escape and of capturing the British ship.

"We were trying to borrow money against the inn. Then we were going to see if we could buy your freedom," Lottie said.

"There was an old woman who came to the prison ships to sell bread and fresh vegetables. She promised me she would mail the letter but that was nearly a year ago," Hannah explained.

"I don't know where the letter was, but we finally got it last week," Lottie said.

"I'm so grateful for your generosity. I know how much the inn means to you. That you would risk it for me is unbelievable," Hannah said.

"You know how much we love you, child," Madeline said with a smile.

Hannah lowered her voice, "Although we could have paid you back because when our ship sank, we buried a chest of Spanish doubloons. When we sail again, we are going to retrieve that treasure."

"A real treasure? How exciting!" Lottie said.

"Some of the money will go to the survivors of the crew that died. Their families probably really need it by now," Hannah said.

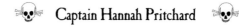

Lottie brushed the hair on Hannah's forehead with a look of motherly concern. "You are so thin, and I see you had the pox."

"Yes, I had smallpox while I was on the prison ship. But thanks to Dobbs, I only had a light case. Many of the men died from it and other diseases. You would not believe how awful it was, Lottie."

"Oh, you poor dear. You have been through so much," Lottie said with great concern.

"Some of your cooking is the only cure I need," Hannah said with an encouraging smile.

Madeline hustled to the kitchen and came back with two heaping plates of food for Hannah and Daniel.

"I was afraid you would be upset with me for leaving without telling you," Hannah admitted.

"We were not upset. We were just terribly worried," Lottie said.

Before much longer, Dobbs and the rest of the crew arrived. They all had one of the inn's wonderful dinners. People from the town drifted in, and soon every chair in the dining room was full. Madeline and Lottie rushed around serving the customers. A serving girl from the neighborhood named Rose, who was round faced and sweet, arrived to help. The new crew sat at a different table drinking glasses of ale and flirting with Rose.

At last, the customers had left, and Hannah, Daniel, and Dobbs sat with Madeline and Lottie. They told of their adventures over the last two years while Rose cleared the other tables.

The door opened and let in a draft of cold wintry air. In wandered the largest man that Hannah had ever seen. He was so tall that he had to duck his head as he entered. For all his size, he was trim, handsome even, Hannah thought. But there was a hard, coldness in his eyes.

"Hello, Lottie my girl. I know it's late, but is there any chance for a meal?"

"I'm not a girl, and I am certainly not your girl," Lottie mumbled under her breath. But out loud she said, "Of course, Captain Cutter."

Captain Cutter wandered off and sat at a table next to the *Hannah*'s crew. Dobbs stood up and shook his hand. "I am Captain Dobbs from the ship last night. You really gave us quite a scare."

"It's a good thing you spoke up when you did. It wouldn't do us any good to fire on our own people," Captain Cutter responded with a broad smile that did not quite reach his eyes.

By the time Madeline and Lottie returned from the kitchen with food, Captain Cutter had moved over to talk to the seamen. He began to regale them with tales of his fights with the British.

"I take it you don't think much of Captain Cutter," Dobbs said when Lottie returned and took a seat at the table. Lottie grimaced.

"No reason really. With the way he brags, you would think he had personally sunk half the British fleet, but there is just something"—she hesitated—"something about him." She laughed, "I suppose I'm being overly dramatic."

Dobbs looked over at the crew. They were listening in rapt attention to Captain Cutter.

"I think we are going to lose part of the crew," Daniel said. "I can't imagine the two who were so sick will be able to talk themselves into another sea voyage."

"John told me that he was worried about his mother," Hannah said. "I think he is homesick."

"We will be signing on a full crew as soon as I can get a commission," Dobbs reassured them.

"Your old room is ready for you," Madeline said to Hannah. "I had Rose fill up the tub for a bath."

"A bath," Hannah exclaimed, while gathering up her packages. "That sounds lovely."

The room was just as she remembered. A warm flannel nightgown was laid out on the bed. The lavender scented bath was ready. She hesitated only for a second and then stepped into the tub.

chapter three

Shares for Survivors

Hannah was anxious to return to sea, but Dobbs warned her that it would be several weeks before the ship was ready for another voyage. Each night, as Dobbs joined them for dinner, his face grew grimmer.

"The American merchants are reluctant to ship things by sea. There have been too many losses. They are sending everything over land," Dobbs said. "I have spoken several times to a naval officer about a commission from the Continental navy, but nothing seems to be happening."

One day, Dobbs approached Hannah. "We need to distribute the money from the sale of the captured ship that Mr. Gaines left," he said. "I want you and Daniel to find as many families as you can and give them their share." He handed Hannah a paper. "These are the addresses that Captain Nelson wrote down when the men originally signed up. Some of them will be hard to find. Hopefully, you can trace their families by talking to the townspeople."

Dobbs handed Hannah a wooden box. "I have divided the money. Each family will get one cloth sack inside this box. Tell them there may be more if we can find where we buried the treasure. I imagine some of the families are in dire need by now."

Hannah nodded gravely. "We will do our best to get the shares to them."

The next morning, Hannah and Daniel went to the livery stable and rented a buggy.

Most of the addresses were close together in a section of town occupied by working men, fishermen, and sailors. They found the first house easily enough. A short, stout woman with a dour face opened the door and eyed them suspiciously.

"Are you Mrs. Pembroke?" Hannah asked.

"Who wants to know?" the woman retorted.

Briefly, Hannah explained their mission. The woman's face softened. "I thought you were a bill collector," she said. She opened the door, allowing them to enter.

Inside, Hannah saw two young women hooking a woolen rug. "We have kept going by selling rugs and quilts," Mrs. Pembroke explained. "I thought my husband was dead," she said heavily. "He had never stayed away this long before. It is good to finally know what happened."

Daniel handed her one of the bags. "I hope this will help," he said.

Although they found the Pembroke residence on their first try, some of the other addresses required diligent detective work. However, by asking neighbors and other relatives, they managed to track down most of the families. When they began handing out the shares, they thought that the project would only take a few days. But after a month, they still had a few names on the list. They continued passing out the bags. Some of the women were tearful, and others seemed like they might be secretly happy. But all of them were pleased to get the money. They had one more name on the list, but when they found the house, a man answered the door.

"We are looking for Mrs. Chase," Hannah explained. "Is she here?"

"Mrs. Chase was evicted six months ago," the man said. "She couldn't pay the rent."

"Do you know where she went?" Daniel asked.

"She owed back rent. The landlord sent her to debtor's prison—she and the children," he added.

Hannah was horrified. "Six months! Where can we find the prison?" she asked.

The man pointed, "Follow this road out of town. You'll see it."

They climbed back in the buggy and drove in silence. A few miles more and they saw a gray stone building completely surrounded by a high fence. Inside the fence, there was not a blade of grass. Some children sat in the dirt listlessly digging with a stick. A guard sat on a bench nearby watching them. He stood up and walked to the fence as Hannah and Daniel approached.

"We are looking for Mary Chase," Hannah said. "Is she being held here?"

The guard nodded but made no move to fetch her. Daniel reached into his pocket and handed the guard a few coins. The guard turned with an indolent stare and called to one of the hollow-eyed, thin children playing in the dirt. She looked about ten. "Mary, go find your mother."

The child got up, and, with a curious stare at Hannah and Daniel, went inside the building. A minute later, she returned with a small woman wearing ragged clothes. With a glance at the guard who positioned himself so that he could hear, she stepped over to the fence.

"Your husband was killed by the British," Daniel said gently. At this moment, the woman burst into tears.

"All this time I thought he had abandoned us. I have been so angry." Seeing her tears, the guard had moved away with a disgusted look.

"We have some money for you," Hannah whispered, starting to hand her the bag through the fence.

Mrs. Chase held up her hand and, with a furtive look at the guard, said, "Someone will steal it. Is there enough to pay my debt?"

"How much is the debt?" Daniel asked.

"Eighty dollars," she answered.

"There is that and more," Hannah said. "There is two hundred dollars."

"My sister lives in Philadelphia. She married well and she would take us in, but I did not have enough money for a stagecoach. Please go to the office in front. Tell them that you are paying my debt."

Hannah and Daniel did as she asked. A man at the desk looked at the money, checked it against the ledger, and sent another man to release Mrs. Chase and her children. A few minutes later, she walked out the door.

"Climb in the buggy," Hannah said, squeezing in to make room. "We will take you to the stagecoach so that you can buy tickets."

Mrs. Chase purchased the tickets. "It leaves at first light in the morning," she said.

"Why don't you buy some clothes?" Hannah suggested. "Then I will take you to the Red Rooster Inn. You can get a bath and a good meal."

Hannah helped her pick out two dresses: one simple cotton and the other wool. She also bought a shawl and each of the children got two outfits.

"I'm afraid that I don't have enough for the inn," Mrs. Chase said looking at her remaining coins.

"You can stay in my room," Hannah said. "I have a feeling my friends Madeline and Lottie will be happy to feed you."

Daniel had already gone to the inn and told Madeline and Lottie about the poor woman's plight. Lottie sat them at a table and dished them up steaming bowls of vegetable soup, hot biscuits, and slices of cheese. The children's eyes widened in delight at the sight of so much food. Hannah's heart ached for them. She hoped that Mrs. Chase's sister would treat them kindly. Rose had already made a bath in Hannah's room for Mrs. Chase. Lottie told Hannah to stay in her room for the night so Mrs. Chase and the children would be able to relax. Hannah ate her dinner alone, unhappy to see that Daniel again sat with Captain Cutter, intently listening to his stories.

Dobbs came in and sat down beside Hannah. "I don't think that the navy officers here in Portsmouth have the authority to give us a commission. If I don't hear something in a few weeks, I will have to go to Philadelphia to plead our case," he said.

After Daniel turned in for the night, Captain Cutter grabbed a chair and, without asking, sat at their table. "I think we should team up," he said to Dobbs. "We could sail together. I have a great idea. There is big money to be made in the slave trade. We could sail together to Africa and pick up a load to sell in the South."

Hannah quickly glanced at Madeline working hard in the kitchen, grateful that she had not heard him.

A look of anger passed over Dobbs's face. "Absolutely not," he said through gritted teeth.

Cutter persisted. "It's not like they are human. They are different from you and me."

Hannah sputtered, "Are you saying that Madeline is not human?"

"Well, there are bound to be a few exceptions," Cutter said. "But overall, men say they are subhuman."

Dobbs interrupted, "I will have no part in this plan."

"Suit yourself," Cutter said. "It was just a simple idea." With that, he left the table and sat with the crew from the *Hannah.* He started another story of his adventures.

Hannah and Daniel had quarreled about Captain Cutter the first morning when they walked to get their shoes.

"He is amazing," Daniel said, his face animated with admiration. "The *Sea Serpent* makes the British crews get into their ship's boats. Then they board the ship, strip it, and then sink it."

"What if the crew does not give up without a fight?" Hannah had asked.

"Then he just blows them out of the water," Daniel responded.

"What about the crews in the ship's boats?"

Daniel shrugged. "I suppose some of them make it safely to land."

"If they had made it to land there would be a big bounty on that ship. Every British ship in the navy would be after it," Hannah said.

"Cutter did say that once they had blown the ship's boats up, too," Daniel responded.

Hannah hated the British, but that did not sound fair. Either the British starved to death or were capsized on the open sea. Or even worse, Captain Cutter and his crew were shooting boatloads of unarmed men.

"How does he make the serpent's eyes glow like they did?" Hannah asked.

"Oh that's a really clever thing," Daniel enthused. "The head is attached so they can reach in and light two small lanterns inside."

Hannah had to admit that it was a clever idea, but she still believed Captain Cutter was evil. "It doesn't sound to me," she said, "like Captain Cutter is a good man."

Daniel bristled. "Good men don't win wars," he said. "I think he is a hero."

"I don't," Hannah said.

They had continued on their way and picked up their new shoes, which did indeed fit perfectly as the cobbler had promised. But Daniel and Hannah had not talked much since then, and Daniel had been sitting with the ship's crew instead of her.

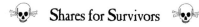

When Hannah awoke the next morning, she found Lottie and Madeline already hard at work in the kitchen. Mrs. Chase and the children sat in the dining room eating a breakfast of honey rolls and coffee.

"I will walk with you to the stage depot," Hannah said, grabbing a roll for herself from the kitchen. Mrs. Chase looked like a different woman already. She chose the wool dress for the journey, and the children were dressed neatly. They had on their new woolen coats as well. Hannah thought the new clothes looked nice. But the real difference was the way the family looked, with hope in their eyes and smiles on their faces. Hannah was touched that she could make such a difference in their lives. She was proud to work for a crew that took care of its own.

Lottie bustled in from the kitchen with a large box. "There is bread, cheese, and an orange in here for each of you."

Mrs. Chase wiped a tear from her face and sighed. "I was beginning to think that there were not kind people left in this world. After the last few months, I did not think we would ever be free. You have no idea how much this all means to me." The children smiled, but they still looked wide-eyed and bewildered from their experiences over the last few months.

Lottie knelt down and gave them each a hug. "Things will be better for you now," she said softly in a kind, motherly voice.

"I was not sure if my sister's husband would feel too kindly toward us as a family whose husband had deserted them. But as a widow, I have a measure of respectability."

Portsmouth was just coming to life as they walked quickly to the stage. Wagons rumbled down the road, and shopkeepers opened their doors for the day.

"You will really enjoy the stagecoach ride," Hannah said to the children as they waited to board. "I rode a stage-coach when I came here. One time, we tipped over and a very fat woman fell right on top of me." The children giggled at the thought, but Mrs. Chase looked alarmed. Hannah smiled. "Everyone pushed it back up, and we were up and moving in a few minutes. No one even got hurt," she said, trying to ease Mrs. Chase's mind.

When the stagecoach arrived, Hannah gave each of them a hug and wished them the best of luck. Mrs. Chase thanked her again and gave her a smile. As they boarded, Mrs. Chase squeezed on to the same seat with her children as other passengers quickly boarded. The horses stomped their hooves, making the harnesses jingle. It was cold enough that their breaths made tiny puffs of steam in the early spring morning air. The driver cracked his whip, and they were off to Philadelphia.

Hannah hoped that they would have a much better life with Mrs. Chase's sister. A sailor's life is a hard one. It was clear to Hannah now that it was not only hard on the sailors, but often their families that they left behind.

After Mrs. Chase and her children left, the weeks crawled by. It was summer now and the days were warm. Hannah had moved into her old room. She helped Madeline in the kitchen and assisted Rose serving the customers. Daniel, too, stayed at the inn repairing the roof and doing other odd jobs to earn his keep.

In August, Dobbs announced that he would be making the trip to Philadelphia to talk to government officials about a commission for the *Hannah*. "I may be gone several weeks," he said.

Hannah sighed in despair. She began to think that they would never get out to sea again. Daniel began talking about farming longingly again.

Dobbs had been gone nearly a month before he finally returned from his journey. Hannah was hard at work kneading loaves of bread. From the roof, she could hear Daniel's hammer as he repaired some torn shingles. She heard Daniel shout and she looked out before Dobbs walked in. Hannah noticed that he appeared very pleased as she dusted the flour off of her hands to greet him.

Dobbs sat down next to Hannah. "We are now officially helping our new navy," he said, while showing her the letter of marque. Hannah knew that this was the document that gave them official status as representatives of the United States, so that they could not be hanged as pirates if captured.

"I have another letter promising to pay for any repairs on our ship if we are attacked. We are to deliver a dispatch to the commander-in-chief of the French forces that have come to help us," Dobbs explained.

"The French are fighting with us?" Hannah asked. "That should make the British weaken their resolve."

Dobbs nodded. "I hope so. The war is not going well for us. Washington's army is small, untrained, and poorly equipped. The British keep sending more and more trained soldiers. Although, I have heard that the colonists try to lure the British away from their supply lines. The British do not like to go too far inland because bands of colonial militia fire on them from hiding spots in the trees and behind rocks. The British troops are trained to march into battle. They do not know how to fight in such hit-and-run fashion."

The next day, Dobbs took Hannah aside. "We have a lot of preparations to tend to before we can sail. We need to order firewood for the stove. Are you sure that you still want to be the cook? You did a fine job, however, with a much larger crew, it will be a lot of work."

"I can handle it," Hannah declared stoutly.

"I will hire a new cabin boy to help you," Dobbs said. "A real boy," he added with a chuckle. He gave Hannah a list of supplies for the kitchen, telling her that she may add whatever she needed.

Hannah made arrangements for salt, pork, beans, and biscuits. She also ordered a barrel of oranges and a barrel of apples, demanding the clerk be sure that there were no rotten ones that would make the others spoil.

Thomas and James from the previous crew would not be going on the next journey with the ship. Thomas and James had both been violently seasick, and Dobbs was not surprised when they decided to take jobs as shipbuilders. That's what they had been doing before they joined the *Hannah*'s crew.

"We are sorry to leave you like this, but the shipbuilder was looking for experienced men, and he pays well. I have to admit, I do like the feeling of solid land under my feet," Thomas said.

"Not everyone is cut out to be a sailor. I understand and wish you well," Dobbs said.

John, another member of the old crew, looked a bit red faced as he announced at dinner that he would not be going on with the rest of the crew either.

"I am worried about my mother," he admitted. "She is all alone, and her health is not good. While I have the money, I am going to buy a horse and go home."

Dobbs stood up and shook his hand. "You were a great help, John. We could not have made our escape without you. I wish you well."

John looked relieved. "I was afraid you would be angry," he confessed.

"Of course not," Dobbs said. "You must do what you think is best."

The next few days, Hannah and Daniel inventoried supplies while Dobbs studied charts and made plans to hire a crew. Now that Dobbs had a job from the new government, he was anxious to sail. Hannah and Daniel were equally anxious to start their next adventure, even though they had enjoyed their stay at the inn.

chapter four

Signing a New Crew

They would be taking a passenger with them. One evening at the inn, a man had approached their table. He was the strangest person Hannah had ever seen. He was five feet tall, and his stomach was so large and round that he could barely cover it with his shirt. He was almost bald, except for a ring of wild curly hair that cradled his face and met his neatly trimmed beard. He looked, Hannah thought, like an overgrown monkey. His eyes, however, looked friendly and intelligent.

"I am Henry Teach," he informed them. "Blackbeard the pirate was my great-grandfather."

Dobbs looked at Mr. Teach. "I am afraid we are not set up for passengers."

"I came overland to see my sister in Portsmouth," the little man explained. "I have not seen her for twenty years. I have never taken an ocean voyage even though I live on the Outer Banks of North Carolina. You do not have to make any special arrangements for me, and I can pay you very well."

Dobbs shrugged. "I suppose you could have one of the officer's rooms," he finally agreed.

Dobbs printed a handbill advertising that he was hiring a crew and posted it at port and in various locations around town, including the saloons. By this time, two more men from the original crew had quit. Dobbs hired a man named Mr. Ames to be the first mate. Mr. Ames had sailed on several ships and was an experienced officer.

Several days before they were ready to sail, Dobbs and Mr. Ames sat at a table on the dock hiring seamen. Some of the applicants looked a bit rough, but Dobbs was more concerned about their experience. At the end of the line were two boys about twelve years old, and they looked exactly the same. Hannah had never seen twins before. Their names were Jonah and Joshua.

"We want to stay together," one of them exclaimed eagerly.

Dobbs hesitated. "And what do your parents say?" he asked.

"We are orphans," the one Hannah thought might be Joshua said. "Our parents died when we were three. For a while, we were at an orphanage, but the last year we have been living on the streets."

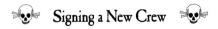

Dobbs nodded, "I will take you both." Dobbs handed them some coins. "Buy yourself two changes of clothes and some boots. You may sleep on the ship until we go."

Thanking him profusely, the boys scampered off.

"You will never see those two boys again," Mr. Ames said.

"I think I will," Dobbs said. "If not, I hope they put the money to good use."

A few days before sailing, Daniel came to Dobbs with a worried look. "Captain Cutter asked me what I knew about the treasure. I think one of the men had too much to drink and mentioned it to him. Thank heavens they do not have any idea where it is."

"Well, that explains why Captain Cutter has been offering to accompany us. After I turned him down to get slaves, I thought he would stay away."

"Slaves?" Daniel questioned.

"Captain Cutter wanted us to go to Africa and pick up a load of slaves," Dobbs said.

Daniel looked shocked. "I didn't know."

"Cutter is not a good man," Dobbs said.

Daniel looked thoughtful. "I am beginning to see that."

Lottie and Madeline had a present for the *Hannah*'s crew. It was a beautiful new American flag to fly on the ship. They unfolded it and held it up proudly. There were red and white stripes and, in one corner, was a circle of creamy white stars sewn into a square of blue cloth.

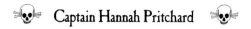

"Each one of the stars stands for one of the thirteen colonies," Lottie explained.

"Thank you," Dobbs said gratefully. "I have been at sea so much that I did not get to see our new flag until I went to Philadelphia. I'm tired of sailing under a false flag. This will show how proud we are to be Americans. I just hope our fellow American ship does not try to follow us. When it comes to a treasure, I'm not sure I would trust Captain Cutter to remember that we are all Americans."

"I have an idea," Daniel said. "If we told Captain Cutter that we were going out to sea for gun practice, he would not follow. By the time he realized that he had been tricked, we would be long gone."

"Wonderful idea," Dobbs agreed. "We will set the date for sailing in one week, but I will require the crew to be onboard for practice. Actually, we could use the practice."

"Why don't we go out twice?" Hannah suggested. "Once for real practice."

"That's a good idea," Dobbs said.

Five days before the official departure, Dobbs sailed the *Hannah* out to open sea. He had managed to round up all of the crew except for one man, who was too drunk to sail with them. Daniel went to show the twins how to be "powder monkeys" by loading the bags of gunpowder and running it to the big guns. Hannah stayed behind and found Mr. Teach to inform him of the early sail. Then she made arrangements for water barrels and some grog for the sailors.

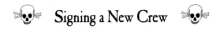

Hannah could hear the steady boom of the guns out at sea. At first, the firings were sporadic, but gradually the firings became steadier. One of the hired men had been a gun captain on another ship and helped to train the men. Hannah walked to the dock. Dobbs had asked her to take charge of the last-minute deliveries. Already, there were crates of chickens and three milking goats. These were at the request of Mr. Teach. He claimed that the British had come to his hometown a year before and taken all their livestock. There was a huge load of firewood for the cook stove and barrels of carrots and turnips to make a good chicken stew. As she checked the deliveries, Captain Cutter approached, his eyes squinting suspiciously.

"Where is your ship?" he demanded.

"Captain Dobbs took it out for gun practice," she said.

Captain Cutter visibly relaxed. "I was worried you had left without saying good-bye," he said.

"We are not sailing for four more days," she replied evenly. "Captain Dobbs might take them out for practice again depending on how they do today."

"You are the cook?" he asked. When Hannah nodded, he said, "You are young to be the cook."

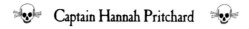

"I was a cabin boy," she said, remembering to lower her voice. "But I was the cook on the way here, and the men seemed to like my cooking."

Captain Cutter looked around and Hannah could see he wasn't interested in cooking.

"Why do you suppose Captain Dobbs won't accept my offer to escort him?" he asked after a minute.

Hannah shrugged. "We have always done quite well by ourselves."

"One member of your crew mentioned something about a treasure?" Captain Cutter inquired.

Hannah forced a laugh. "Treasure? There is supposed to be Blackbeard's treasure hidden at Ocracoke, but people have been looking for that for fifty years. Even his great-grandson doesn't know where it is, or if it really exists."

Captain Cutter interrupted, "Were you not a member of the crew on the *Sea Hawk*?"

Hannah nodded. "Aye, she went down with the captain and most of the crew."

"I heard that there was a huge treasure on the *Sea Hawk*," Captain Cutter said.

Hannah stared at him for a moment. How could he know this, she thought to herself. "It went down with the ship," she lied.

Cutter looked at her for a long time without speaking, as though taking her measure. "Then why did the seaman talk about treasure?" he asked, his eyes narrowing again.

Hannah shrugged again, trying to seem nonchalant. "Maybe he overheard us talking about the lost treasure and thought that we would be looking for it, but he is going to be disappointed."

Captain Cutter strode away without speaking another word. Hannah could not be certain if she had convinced him or not.

That night at dinner, Captain Cutter sat at their table.

"So, how did gun practice go?" he asked.

"Pretty well," Dobbs answered. "But I will give them another day of practice."

"My men are well trained. They could do the fighting for you," Captain Cutter said. "I am beginning to think that you are planning on some secret mission."

Dobbs laughed easily. "Your goal is to sink British ships, which is commendable. But I am not comfortable with the fact that there are never any survivors. Many of the sailors on British ships have been pressed into service—kidnapped from their homes or taken from other ships. I don't think they should all die. Besides, we have accepted a job from the Continental navy. We will fight but only if need be."

Captain Cutter seemed ready to say something else, but instead, he pushed his chair away. “As you wish, but you are making a mistake,” he said curtly.

When he was finally gone, Dobbs sighed. “I hope we do not run into him again. We leave tomorrow, before first light.”

chapter five

Sneaky Escape

A cold wind blew across the deserted streets, as Hannah and a grumpy Mr. Teach hurried to the wharf. It was three in the morning. Hannah had said her farewells to Lottie and Madeline, promising to see them soon.

Lottie had cried, "It seems like we just got you back and here we are saying our good-byes again already."

Hannah hugged Madeline and Lottie. "I will be back. This is home to me, and you are my family."

"Take care of that nice-looking boy Daniel," Madeline said with a wink. Hannah stuck out her tongue playfully as she waved good-bye.

The last of the supplies were being loaded as they reached the dock. A smartly dressed Mr. Ames greeted them as they boarded.

"Welcome aboard, Mr. Teach." Mr. Ames motioned for a sailor to carry Mr. Teach's luggage to a comfortable room that was originally meant for a ship's officer.

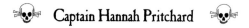

Hannah received a room for herself in the officers' quarters, and she was pleased that it had its own necessary. A sitting stool had been built in one corner above the sea. When not in use, a wooden lid fit over it, and it could be used as a chair.

The twins were already asleep in the small room off the galley. The room was small, barely big enough for two hammocks and a box for their belongings. Hannah peeked in but did not wake them. Even before she had stowed her belongings, Hannah heard the grate of the capstan pulling up the anchor. The sails were unfurled, and the ship moved slowly out of the harbor toward the open sea.

The sea was choppy and Hannah felt her stomach turn uneasily. She made her way to the galley and lit the cook stove after several tries. The twins came out of their room, rubbing their eyes. One of them looked miserable, his face ghostly pale.

"Jonah?" she guessed. "Do you feel sick?" When the boy nodded, she sent him up to the main deck for fresh air. Hannah set out all the supplies needed to make breakfast, then she went to check on the twins. Jonah still looked pale, but the fresh air did seem to revive him.

"Let me show you how to care for the animals," she said. "That was my favorite part of the job when I was a cabin boy."

She showed them how to clean, water, and feed the chickens, and then sent Joshua to fetch a wooden bucket. "Have you ever milked a goat before?"

"No," the boys said, shaking their heads.

She showed them how to wash the teats, and then she sat the wooden bucket underneath and demonstrated how to milk. A steady stream went into the bucket.

"Let me try," said an eager Joshua.

It took both boys several tries, but finally they filled the bucket. Jonah carried the bucket of milk carefully down the galley steps. Then Hannah filled four small pitchers and set trays for Dobbs, Mr. Ames, and Mr. Teach. She set a bowl of porridge on each tray along with the milk and poured each one a cup of coffee. The boys headed for the officers' dining room to deliver the trays. In the meantime, Hannah delivered the porridge and remaining milk to the crew members.

After everyone had been fed, Hannah put the twins to work scrubbing the pots. Both boys had discovered Mr. Grindle's carpentry shop while exploring the ship, and they could talk of little else.

"Mr. Grindle has all kinds of interesting tools and wood," Joshua said excitedly.

Jonah set a clean pot back on the stove. "He said he could teach us some things and help us make a box for our belongings."

"It sounds like you boys would rather be carpenters than cooks," Hannah joked.

The boys hung their heads. "No, no! We like helping you," Joshua said.

"But it would be fun to work with wood," Jonah added. After the pots were cleaned to her satisfaction, she allowed them to go for a short time.

At daybreak, Dobbs assembled the crew on deck. "You do the honors," he said to Daniel, handing him the neatly folded American flag. Daniel attached the flag and ran the pulley to hoist it high. The men cheered.

"We are carrying a letter of marque from the Continental Congress. The French are aiding us in the war effort. Our first task is to take a message to the French army camped at Newport, Rhode Island. Our hold is full of equipment to be delivered at Ocracoke along with our guest, Mr. Teach," Dobbs said.

A hush fell over the men. Hannah saw several of them stare up at the flag. Even the roughest of them seemed to stand straighter and look prouder.

Hannah looked over the new crew gathered together for the flag ceremony. Many of them were hard men with weathered, leathery skin. Their teeth were either missing or black, and their clothes were dirty and ragged. But they were experienced, and they knew exactly what to do, even before Mr. Ames directed them. Other crew members were younger and possibly looking for adventure. They watched the more experienced sailors, eager and excited. To a man, they all respected Captain Dobbs and the first mate. Mr. Ames was the perfect first mate. Calm and firm, he relayed the captain's orders to the men.

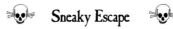

Hannah headed back down to the galley, and Daniel followed her.

"You were right about Cutter," Daniel said. "He is not a good man. I've been thinking about the British crew being left adrift. No one deserves to die that way—not even the British."

Hannah smiled, glad to have her friend back.

Hannah set a large piece of salt pork in a pot of fresh water to soak out some of the salt. Then she fetched a chicken and dispatched it by wringing its neck. She dropped it in a pot of boiling water. Then, taking it out of the pot, she set the twins to work on plucking the feathers.

"P-hew, it smells awful!" Jonah complained.

Hannah chuckled. The boiling water made the feathers easier to pluck, but it also made them smell.

"I'll bet we wouldn't do this if we were real navy men," Joshua grumbled.

Hannah laughed again. "You might," she said.

Cooking for a large crew was harder than Hannah had thought it would be. By the time the last pot had been scrubbed, she was ready for bed. She had fed the men and made a stew for Dobbs, Mr. Ames, and Mr. Teach. The rest she gave to the twins knowing that they had not had a good meal in a long time. Dobbs had called for another gun practice that afternoon, and Hannah could see that the twins were exhausted. She sent them to bed and carried Dobbs his nightly cup of tea.

Dobbs was studying his charts as usual, and Daniel was with him.

Daniel looked at Hannah and smiled. "Captain Dobbs is teaching me how to read charts."

Hannah put the tea down and headed for her own room. As she passed Mr. Teach's room, she could hear the soft, sweet music of a violin.

The *Hannah,* hugging the coast, sailed south. They kept a wary eye out for British ships but saw nothing larger than a fishing boat. If Dobbs's calculations were correct, they should be heading straight for the bay at Rhode Island.

It was Sunday. On every good ship, sailors were not allowed on deck through the week unless they had a chore to do. Although, a sailor who wanted to be outside could often find an excuse to work on the main deck—lengths of rope to be braided or some other pressing chore. However, on Sundays, the crew was allowed on deck. Even though it was cold, men played cards and enjoyed their extra glass of grog. A few tried fishing over the rail.

Two men who had been playing cards on an overturned crate suddenly started to argue. One of the men stood up. There was the flash of a knife. Mr. Ames was there instantly, his hand closing over the wrist of the man holding the knife.

"Drop it," he said tersely. The knife clattered to the deck. "This is a lashable offense," Mr. Ames said, his voice even again. "But Captain Dobbs is not fond of lashing. However, I will be keeping the knife, and you two will not play cards together again during this voyage. If there are any other problems, we will drop you off at the first port."

Mr. Teach came out of his room with his violin in hand and sat down. He began to play a sweet, lilting melody. Several men stopped to listen, and one of them disappeared into his room and returned with a music pipe. Mr. Teach played a more lively song, and the sailor with the pipe joined in, playing with gusto. One of the men named Charles, who had almost no teeth, went to the crew's quarters and returned with a flute. His cheeks flushing crimson, he began to play along with the others.

The men hooted. "A flute Charles? You play the flute?"

"Me mother taught me," Charles growled in response.

By now, there was a good crowd around them. Linking arms, several of the men began to dance a jig accompanied by the lively music. Daniel and Hannah had been playing checkers. They walked over to join the other listeners, leaving the board for the twins. Daniel linked his elbow around Hannah's and swung her around. The men danced until they fell to the deck exhausted and laughing. Mr. Ames leaned against the rail smoking a pipe, talking to Dobbs, and even they looked relaxed.

The sea was calm now. Although the day was cool, the sun was bright. Even though Mr. Ames periodically sent crewmen up the mast to check the horizon, there had been no sign of the *Sea Serpent* or any British vessels. Hannah wished all days could be this much fun.

chapter six

A Message Delivered

It was a dreary, misty morning when they approached Newport, Rhode Island. The crew dropped anchor, and they lowered the smaller ship's boat. Dobbs was to deliver the dispatch. He turned to Mr. Ames. "You are in charge of the ship while I am gone." Then he called for Hannah and Daniel. "You two can row the boat and accompany me."

It was unusually cold for fall. Hannah's fingers, even with the woolen gloves, grew so numb that she could hardly hold on to the oars. Her feet felt like frozen blocks of ice.

Dobbs huddled in the middle of the boat, shaking with cold. "I asked you to row me thinking you might enjoy seeing the French encampment," he said. "I didn't know it would be this miserable."

"It's all right," Daniel answered for the both of them. "We are curious to see the French."

As they rounded a bend, they could see an ocean of tents stretching as far as the eye could see. Most of them were small with an occasional larger one scattered within. Hannah thought that this indicated a higher-ranking soldier. There were small fires built throughout the camp, and men were huddled around each of them fighting for the heat coming from the flames. As they got closer, she could see that one of the larger tents was a cook tent. Men stood impatiently in line waiting for their turn to eat, while other men left with what she could only guess was soup. Even though these troops were clearly off duty, Hannah sensed their alertness. They were clearly a well-disciplined army.

They docked the small boat at the town's wharf. The French encampment was a short distance away. Daniel and Hannah waited at the shore while Dobbs made arrangements to rent a horse and buggy. "The fellow that I rented the horse from said that Rochambeau, the commander-in-chief, is staying in a large brick house near the encampment," Dobbs said when he returned.

They set out at a lively pace passing the huge campsite. "There seem to be a lot of French here," Daniel remarked.

"I was told that there are nearly six thousand officers and soldiers here ready to help us fight," Dobbs said.

They found the large brick mansion with several sharply dressed sentries outside. On one side of the mansion, French soldiers marched in perfect unison. Another group practiced musket fire. Hannah watched with interest. The last row poured powder into the muskets, the row ahead tamping it down. The front row knelt on one knee, aimed, and fired. As soon as the front row had fired, the middle row would move up in front of them and the back row to the middle so that the firings continued without pause. Several officers watched from horseback as the sergeants directed the men. Even though Hannah did not understand the French language, she knew that the officers intended to make the men move even faster than they were.

Hannah admired the precision of the drills and the neat uniforms of the lieutenants. The shirts were white, and their jackets were sky blue. They also wore black fuzzy hats with large feathers popping out of the front. She wondered if the American army looked anywhere near as good. The only soldiers that she had seen wore ragged clothes and had not had much formal training. But the French infantrymen wore white uniforms, with a white sash, and a three-cornered hat with a jaunty feather and a blue jacket.

They climbed out of the wagon and explained their mission to the guard at the door. The guard rapped on the door and spoke to another soldier before returning to his post. Hannah wished that she could understand the words of the musical French language. A minute later, the door opened.

"Commander-in-Chief Rochambeau will see you now," the soldier said in perfect English. They followed the soldier to a large office furnished with velvet chairs and damask wall coverings. Commander-in-Chief Rochambeau adjusted his powdered wig, stood up, and bowed slightly.

"I am Jean-Baptiste Donatien de Vimeur, comte de Rochambeau, commander-in-chief of the French forces in America. How may I help you?"

Dobbs offered his hand to introduce himself. "I am Captain Dobbs of the ship *Hannah*. I bring a dispatch."

Rochambeau took Dobbs's hand. "It's a pleasure to meet you."

Rochambeau was a tall and stately-looking man, with a firm chin and an intelligent face. He appeared to be about fifty years old. His jacket was embellished with gold on the shoulder and sleeve. A wide red sash was draped across his chest. Hannah had never seen George Washington (the leader of the Continental Army) before, but she hoped that he was as impressive-looking as Rochambeau. His regal bearing demanded respect.

Dobbs motioned to Hannah and Daniel. "These are two of my crewmen, Daniel and Jack."

"How do you do?" Hannah and Daniel said together.

Rochambeau did not offer to shake hands with them. He picked up a bell from his desk and rang it. Instantly, a warm, motherly-looking woman appeared at the door.

"Martha, some tea"—and then he hesitated— "coffee?" When they nodded, he turned back to Martha. "Some coffee for our guests."

"Right away, sir," she said with an American accent.

"Sit down," Rochambeau said as he motioned toward the regal velvet furniture. Hannah looked around. She had never been in such an elegant home. Martha returned carrying a large silver tray. She handed each of them a steaming cup of coffee and a napkin. She set a plate of small, square, decorated cakes on the desk before hurrying away. Rochambeau offered each of them a cake.

Daniel bit into his, "Mmm . . . these are delicious."

Rochambeau almost cracked a smile. "I will give your compliments to Mrs. Watson. She is learning to be a real French cook."

Hannah chewed her cake slowly. It tasted delicious. It was soft and sweet. She wondered how Mrs. Watson had made the tiny flower decorations on the top.

Dobbs cleared his throat. "General Washington would like to have a meeting with you to discuss how best to utilize your troops when he takes back New York City."

Rochambeau frowned. "I am not sure New York should be our first priority," he said thoughtfully. "I am thinking that Virginia would be a better idea, although I don't believe that your general will agree with me. We believe that the British fleet is slowly moving toward New York, which will make it even more difficult to take." He stopped and looked at Dobbs. "Where are you heading from here?"

"To the Carolinas," Dobbs replied, "with a load of supplies for the colonial militia."

"Be very watchful," Rochambeau cautioned. "If you follow the coast south you may run into British ships heading north."

"Thank you for the warning," Dobbs said.

"Our French fleet is coming, but unfortunately they have been delayed," Rochambeau said.

"We are happy to have the French on our side," Dobbs said.

"Your statesman, Benjamin Franklin, went to France to ask for our help. Franklin is a witty and eloquent speaker. At least, when you can keep him away from the ladies, that is," Rochambeau said.

Hannah was embarrassed that she had never heard of Benjamin Franklin, but she did not say a word.

"You have the dispatch for me?" Rochambeau asked, holding out his hand.

Dobbs handed him a large envelope filled with papers. "These are from the Continental Congress."

Rochambeau broke the seal and shuffled through the papers. "Thank you for bringing these. I'm sure General Washington and I can come up with a plan." Rochambeau walked with them to the door, and Hannah peered around trying to see as much of the elegant house as she could. Exquisite chandeliers hung from high ceilings, and thick woven rugs covered the polished wood floors. Rochambeau noticed Hannah's curiosity.

"It is a lovely house, is it not?" Rochambeau asked. Hannah blushed, embarrassed to be caught gawking. But Rochambeau just smiled. "It belonged to a Tory. I take it your countrymen convinced him to move to London—something to do with tar and feathers."

As they drove the wagon back to the ship, Daniel whispered to Hannah, "I would feel like I had to tiptoe around in a fancy house like that."

Hannah nodded. "I don't think I would like to be that rich, although it would be nice to have a cook and a maid to do all the work."

Daniel poked her with his elbow. "You would just be bored if you didn't have any work to do."

"You're probably right," Hannah said. She rubbed her hands together quickly to try to warm them from the brisk wind that swept over the bay.

Once they were back on the ship, Dobbs said, "I had planned on following the coast south. But if Rochambeau is correct, I think we will be smart to head out farther into the open sea. We have completed one part of our task."

As they watched the small boat being raised to the deck, Dobbs said, "After we get these arms and supplies to the patriots in the Carolinas, we can tend to our business."

"Do you think we can find the treasure?" Hannah whispered.

Dobbs shook his head. "I hope we can. I only have a vague idea of where we were when we capsized. When the British captured us, they put us in the hold so that I couldn't see any points of reference. I think we were South of Ocracoke, however."

They sailed without incident. Dobbs had several small gun practices, and they could now load and aim the guns in less than three minutes. The twins proved to be hard workers and cheerful companions. During their free time, they disappeared into Mr. Grindle's shop. Both boys loved working with wood.

"Maybe me and my brother can open up a furniture shop," Jonah said.

The two boys were very much alike, but Jonah was more thoughtful, somewhat of a dreamer. Joshua was more impulsive. Sometimes Hannah had to scold him for not being thorough about his chores. Once he had forgotten to water the goats, and several times she had to send him back to rescrub pots. Even though the boys had lived on the streets, they had not lost their goodness.

chapter seven

Fire and Ice

As they headed out to the open sea, the weather became colder by the hour. Dobbs had decided to sail east into the open ocean to avoid the British ships before turning south.

"We were fortunate not to run into any British patrols," Dobbs told Hannah and Daniel. "But we do not want to push our luck too much. With some distance from the coast, we should be safer when we head south."

The sea was choppy but not enough to cause problems. The cold was bitter, and the men grumbled and complained when they had chores that sent them outside. Hannah helped the twins cover the chicken crates with oilcloth and gave the animals extra straw. The galley was the warmest place on the ship. Everyone found some excuse to spend a few minutes there huddled around the stove. The twins returned from delivering meals shaking with cold. Dobbs had purchased them heavy wool coats and hats, but they didn't seem to help much. They sat at the worktable until they stopped shivering.

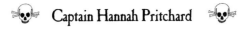

"Where did you learn to cook Jack?" Jonah asked.

Hannah stirred the beans for the crew. "My mother taught me and Dobbs, too." The twins looked at her in amazement.

"Captain Dobbs was a cook?" Joshua asked.

Hannah nodded. "And the ship's doctor. The captain can do any job on this ship."

Jonah carefully peeled the potatoes. "Looks like you know your way around a kitchen," Hannah observed.

"We worked in the kitchen at the orphanage," Joshua told her. "The matron at the orphanage was nice to us. Sometimes she made us cookies. One day," Joshua said, continuing the story, "a man and woman came to the orphanage. Their name was Taggard. They wanted to adopt a boy. They seemed very nice, and they agreed to take both of us. But when we got to their house, they locked us in a shed. We didn't even have a bed—just some straw and a thin blanket."

Jonah nodded as he picked up another potato. "They made us work all day, and they only gave us watery soup to eat. Then they would lock the shed at night. When they said that we were working too slowly, they gave us three lashes each with a whip. Then, for extra punishment, we had to go to bed without supper."

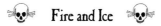

"Another time we were told to unload a wagon, but instead we just ran away," Joshua interrupted.

"You poor boys!" Mr. Teach said from the doorway. He had come in and overheard the story. "Did they educate you at the orphanage?" he asked.

The boys shook their heads.

"You can't read?" Hannah asked.

Again, the boys shook their heads.

"This situation must be corrected," Mr. Teach declared. "Among my luggage there are new slates and primers that I am bringing back for our children." He looked at Hannah. "Can you spare the boys for a couple hours a day?"

"We don't need to read," Joshua said. "Mr. Grindle says that when we get back to port he has a friend who might take us on as apprentices."

"A carpenter still needs to read," Mr. Teach argued. "How will you read a customer's order, measure correctly, or write up a bill of sale?"

"Can you read, Jack?" Jonah asked Hannah.

"Of course," Hannah said. "The only book that we had at home was the Bible. I would like to read some other books someday."

"I have a wonderful book of Greek myths," Mr. Teach told her. "I will lend it to you. The Greeks believed that there were many gods and goddesses, but they gave them human foibles."

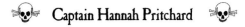

"But that is blasphemy," Hannah protested.

"The ancient Greeks truly believed that, but we just read them as stories. These stories date back to before the New Testament was written. I also have a book of plays by a man named William Shakespeare. Some of them are quite witty."

Mr. Teach stayed in the warm galley while Hannah prepared dinner. She made sure that the twins bundled up in their warm coats and hats before sending them with trays of food to Dobbs and Mr. Ames. The twins returned a few minutes later trembling with cold. Their noses were red, and they said it had started to rain.

"It's freezing on the deck and very slippery," Joshua told them. The rain continued as darkness fell.

"Come on in," Mr. Teach said, deciding that it was a good time for a lesson. He sat with the twins at the small wooden table as the rain continued. Then, Daniel burst through the door. Tiny icicles covered his hair and clothes.

"You know those storms at home that covered all the trees with ice?" Daniel asked. Hannah nodded. "That is happening to the ship—the sails, the deck, and the railings. Everything is covered with ice." Suddenly, there was a dreadful cry from up above.

"Man overboard!"

"You all stay here. There is nothing that you can do," Daniel said.

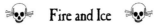

Ignoring Daniel's order, Hannah put on her coat and pushed open the galley hatch.

"Get down below!" Dobbs thundered. "We don't need anyone else sliding off into the ocean." There was enough moonlight left that Hannah could see the thick covering of ice. She could hear men frantically chopping at the ice trying to free the ship's boat for rescue.

A few minutes later, Dobbs shouted, "It's too late! In water like this, he would be dead by now. Get below." The twins and Mr. Teach, pale faced, looked at Hannah.

Hannah stood by the galley hatch. "You can't just give up!" she screamed.

Dobbs looked down at her. "Jack, he is dead. A person could not last more than a minute or two in that kind of cold water."

"Life is fleeting," Mr. Teach said philosophically. "One never knows how much time he really has. I guess the trick is to try to live each day the best you possibly can. That way, when you die, you don't have to think that I wish I would have been kinder to this person, or apologized to that person, or simply said I love you to another."

Hannah looked at Mr. Teach with newfound respect. "That is good advice," she said.

Mr. Teach looked embarrassed. "Really, it's just too bad that fellow who just drowned was not more like my great-grandfather, Blackbeard."

"What do you mean?" Jonah asked.

"When Blackbeard was captured, they cut off his head and tied it to the bow of the ship. Then they just tossed his body into the sea. The legend claims that he was so angry that his body swam around the ship three times before it finally sank."

Jonah's eyes were wide. "Is that true?"

Mr. Teach chuckled. "Legends are usually a great exaggeration."

"We thought that we were going to be real pirates when we joined the ship," Joshua admitted.

"Real pirates are a rather nasty bunch," Mr. Teach said. "They rob and steal from everyone. Sometimes, they hold women and children for ransom. They have a good system of operations, however. They vote for a captain, and then they have a system of shares for the spoils."

"As far as the British are concerned, we are pirates," Hannah said. "We would be pirates, except for the letter of marque we carry that states we represent our government. We could be hanged as pirates if we attack a British ship."

"Really?" Joshua asked breathlessly.

Hannah nodded. "Captain Dobbs, Daniel, and I were captured. We were prisoners of war. Life on the British prison ships was terrible, but at least we were not hanged. They put us on these old, rundown ships, where even the food was rotten—slimy vegetables, meat with maggots, and weevils in the porridge."

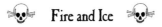

The boys looked solemn, so Hannah said quickly, "Privateers operate just like pirates. We chose Dobbs to be captain, and we all have shares in any profit."

"Even us?" Joshua asked.

"Even you," Hannah assured him. "Cabin boys get half a share. However, because there are two of you, that's a whole share."

"What about the man who fell overboard?" Joshua asked in a hushed tone.

"Captain Dobbs will see that his family, if he has any, gets his share." Hannah sent the twins to bed leaving their door open so that some of the warmth from the galley could creep inside.

"I am not sure that we can safely make it across the deck to our rooms," Mr. Teach said. He was lying under the table using his coat for a pillow. Hannah decided to copy his idea stretching out before the stove. She thought that she would not be able to sleep, but the next thing she knew, it was morning. She needed to use the necessary in her room, but when she tried to open the galley hatch, it didn't budge. She banged at it with the side of her hand, but nothing happened. After a few minutes of shouting and banging, she heard Mr. Ames's voice.

"Hang on!" Mr. Ames shouted. "We'll get you chipped out. Stand back!"

She could hear men chipping at the ice covering the crew's quarters so they could change shift. Mr. Teach stood up, rubbing his eyes. The twins stumbled out of their hammocks. Hannah stoked up the fire in the stove, added wood, and set water to boil for coffee. At last, she heard men working on the galley door.

As soon as it was free, Hannah stepped out into a crystal wonderland. The air was still cold, but the sun was shining. Every inch of the ship was covered in sparkling ice. Long icicles hung down from the rails and rigging. Someone had tied a rope to the quarterdeck stairs, and, by holding on, Hannah was able to walk across the slippery ice without falling.

The ship was scarcely moving. The sails were covered with ice and could not pick up the breeze. She made it to her room and used the necessary, grateful that it was inside. The two on the deck were enclosed in stalls, but there was no ceiling. She imagined the seats were covered with ice. No one would be occupying those for very long.

"All my years at sea, I've never seen anything this bad," Dobbs said. "We can chip the ice away from most things, but not the sails. The weight of the ice has already torn them, and it looks like the top of the mizzenmast is cracked."

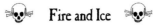

"Let's hope the sun is warm enough to melt the ice the farther south we go," Hannah said.

"I wanted to stay away from the coast, but I think we will have to set out for the Chesapeake Bay. There is a shipyard there where we can make repairs," Dobbs said.

"I think the ship looks beautiful," Hannah offered.

Dobbs chuckled. "It would be beautiful if it were someone else's ship."

That Sunday, there was no breeze. The ship was almost becalmed. The sea looked like a shimmering plate of glass. It was only slightly warmer, but most of the ice had begun to melt. Despite the bitter cold, the sailors gathered on deck, wrapped in their coats and hats. Mr. Teach did not play his violin, as his fingers were too numb.

Charles, the sailor who played the flute, approached Hannah. "I will try to catch us a big fish or two," he said. "No offense lad, but a man gets mighty tired of salt pork."

"If you catch them, I will cook them," Hannah said.

"I need to find some bait," Charles said.

"Maybe the fish will find salt pork to their liking," Hannah said with a mischievous grin. Laughing, Hannah made her way to the galley and cut Charles several hunks of salt pork. Charles fastened them to a large hook. The hook was tied to a length of twine. Hannah did not have much faith in the crude contraption, but she watched with interest for several minutes before returning to the galley.

She counted out enough oranges for each man to have one and returned to the deck to pass them out.

Hannah handed Charles his orange. "No luck?" she asked.

"Well, I guess the fish don't like your salt pork either," Charles said teasingly.

Hannah laughed, but just then there was a mighty tug on the line that almost pulled Charles over the rail. His half-eaten orange rolled across the deck and was quickly forgotten.

"Got something big!" he shouted, and immediately other sailors offered him advice.

"Let it run and then pull it back," one man who had experience on a fishing boat said. "You have to get it tired."

"What if it's a shark?" Jonah said, straining to see the dark shape under the water.

"They are good to eat, too," someone else answered.

"But what about all of those teeth. If we pull it on deck, it could bite us," Jonah insisted.

Just then, the fish made a mighty leap coming clear out of the water.

"It's a swordfish," a sailor named Ivan shouted. "At least two hundred pounds, maybe more."

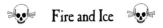

Although it was still cold, Charles had sweat dripping down his face. As the battle continued, hour after hour, Hannah wondered who was more tired, Charles or the fish.

"I am not sure the line is strong enough to pull it up on to the ship," Daniel remarked.

"I know," Charles said through gritted teeth.

Mr. Ames and Dobbs leaned over the rail, watching the contest with the rest of the crew.

Mr. Ames straightened up. "I saw something that would work in the weapons chest," he said, as he sprinted off to fetch it. He returned a minute later with a triumphant look and a large hook in his hand. "Coax the fish up close enough where I can get a good throw," he yelled.

Charles slowly rewound the line, forcing the fish near the side of the ship. Mr. Ames threw the hook across the top of the fish, then quickly drew it in until the barb sunk deep into the fish. The men cheered as Mr. Ames pulled on the rope tied to the hook, and Charles pulled on the twine until they pulled it over the rail and onto the main deck. The fish thrashed violently across the deck as men leaped out of the way. Hannah almost felt sorry for it as the last bit of fight left it, and it was finally still.

"There you go, Jack," Charles said wearily. "Something besides salt pork for dinner."

Hannah looked at the fish. It was nearly as big as a man. "I don't know how to clean it," she confessed softly.

There was a flash of knives as several men stepped forward to clean the large fish. An hour later, the fish had been gutted, deboned, and cut into huge steaks.

"Go peel potatoes," Hannah told the twins, who had been watching with wide eyes the whole time. "Tonight, we will have a feast," she said.

Hannah set the pan on the stove and put some lard to melt in it. The swordfish steaks were on the table. She counted them out, making sure she had a good portion for each man and even some extra for those who wanted it.

Suddenly, she smelled smoke and turned to see the grease had gotten too hot. Without thinking, she grabbed the pan. But the handle was too hot, and she dropped it just as the grease burst into flames. Tongues of fire shot across the floor and up the wall. Fire was the worst thing that could happen on a wooden ship. It could spread quickly, fueled by timber and pitch used to seal the boards. For a second, Hannah stood horrified watching the flames.

"Fire!" she screamed. She picked up the bucket of sand and threw it on the flames that were licking around her feet. The flames were smothered but still continued to burn on the walls. She took a large measuring cup and filled it with water from the boiling pot of potatoes and splashed it against the wall just as several sailors burst into the galley. The last of the flames flickered and died.

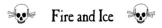

Hannah sat down heavily. Her beautiful galley was a mess, and she had endangered the whole crew. She buried her face in her hands. Dobbs arrived and sent the men to dip buckets of water from the sea.

"We can't take a chance of any hot spots flaring up when no one is around," Dobbs said.

"I am so sorry," Hannah managed to choke out. "I was so careless."

Dobbs patted her shoulder. "I had a fire or two in my cooking days," he confessed. "One of them was worse than this. At least you acted quickly."

Hannah felt a bit better as she watched the men drench the galley, turning it into a mess of dirty water and wet sand.

"Go ahead and cook the fish," Dobbs said. "Clean the galley later. Save as much sand as you can."

Hannah nodded. When she served the men a heaping platter of golden brown, carefully tended fish steaks and boiled potatoes, the men teased her unmercifully.

"Don't ever ask Jack to cook anything but salt pork," Charles cackled loudly. "He gets so mad he tries to burn down the whole ship."

"We love your salt pork," the men chorused.

"Good!" Hannah said, trying to joke back. "You'll be eating that from now on."

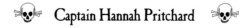

The twins, who had been taking a lesson from Mr. Teach when the fire started, were aghast when they saw the mess. But they gamely swept up the sand and carefully dumped it back into the bucket. By the time they went to bed, the only remainder of the nearly disastrous event was a few scorched spots on the smooth wooden floors.

chapter eight

An Attack, and a Rescue

The next day, there was enough wind to finally resume their journey. Except for a few tears, the sails seemed to work. But the ropes had snapped in several places on the rigging, and Dobbs would not let anyone climb them for fear more had been weakened. Dobbs assembled the crew and held a service for the sailor who had fallen overboard. Hannah did not know him, although she remembered that he was one of the two men arguing about cards. He had pulled a knife out of his pocket before Mr. Ames had intervened.

Without being able to adjust the sails, it was very hard to maneuver the ship. However, with the steady breeze, they were finally making some progress.

The twins were getting along well with their lessons. "They are bright little lads," Mr. Teach said, when he gave Hannah the promised book of Greek myths. She was immediately engrossed in the book. She wondered how people could believe in gods with such human foibles as jealousy, anger, and deceit. The stories fascinated her, and, every second that she was not working, she had her nose in the book.

"That book must be very good. You never have time to talk to me anymore," Daniel complained.

"You should ask Mr. Teach if you can read it when I am done," Hannah said.

Mr. Teach gave Daniel the Shakespeare book.

"How is it?" Hannah asked that Sunday over their usual game of checkers. Daniel made a face and shrugged.

"The stories are all right, but they talk funny. It is hard to read. It's like being in school," he grumbled.

"I am almost done with my book," Hannah said. "I think you will like it."

When they reached the Chesapeake Bay area, Dobbs guided the ship around a small island. Carefully testing each step on the rigging, Daniel climbed partially up the main mast.

"There are two British ships heading north," he shouted. "But I think that they are too far away to cause any problems." He looked the other direction. "There are too many trees to see anything this way, but I think it is clear. Should I climb higher?"

"No," Dobbs answered. "I don't trust that rigging. We will take our chances."

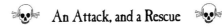

They sailed across the open water at the mouth of the bay. Suddenly, they saw a large British ship sailing directly toward them.

"All right men, man your guns," Dobbs shouted. "But don't fire unless we must. We don't want those other ships to turn around and come after us. Daniel, come down from there."

Daniel scrambled down as the *Hannah* headed for the open bay. There was a loud boom and a puff of smoke from the British ship, but the cannonball dropped before reaching the *Hannah.*

"We are out of range," Daniel gave a gleeful shout. The British ship, however, had caught a current and closed the distance.

"Fire when ready," Dobbs said.

Mr. Ames shouted the order to the gun crews and, one after another, the *Hannah*'s guns fired. Two of the balls went wild, but a third struck the British ship high on the bow. An answering volley came immediately. The first shot took out the head, or the ship's bathroom, before dropping into the ocean. The second ball hit the top of the main mast shattering it into large splinters that rained down on the deck. The new American flag fluttered down, twisted among the torn sails. Hannah raced across the deck and freed it.

Cradling it to her chest, she ran to the galley hatch and down the steps. The *Hannah*'s gunners set off another volley. This time they had found their target, but the British ship had not given up. The bay was still a good distance away, and the *Hannah,* with half of her main mast destroyed and most of the sails torn down, was sluggish and hard to maneuver. A ball hit the ship and Hannah heard screams and shouts from below. Placing the flag on the table, she headed down to grab the medical box. Mr. Teach was already reaching for the box of emergency supplies.

"Captain Dobbs told me that the galley might be the safest spot on the ship. However, I have done some doctoring on the island. I can help with the wounded," Mr. Teach said.

Just then, one of the gunners burst in holding his badly burned hand.

"I need grease!" he cried out.

Hannah reached for the lard but Mr. Teach shouted, "No, wait." Spying a bucket of cold water he said, "Put your hand in there." The sailor hesitated only a second before he plunged his hand in, almost instantly a look of relief flooded his face.

"It does help!" the gunner exclaimed while starting to withdraw his hand.

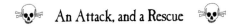

"No, no," Mr. Teach cautioned. "Leave it in the cold water. We will go and help the others and see how you are when we're done."

In the crew's quarters, nearly empty with so many of the men at the guns, they found two men peppered with splinters from the strike. Both were in pain but not seriously injured. Hannah and Mr. Teach pulled out slivers of wood from their skin and rubbed on salve. One of the men had a large chunk of wood embedded into his back. Hannah gingerly pulled it out. The sailor groaned, but did not cry out. The wound was bleeding, and Hannah tried to staunch the flow with some clean gauze. But Mr. Teach stopped her hand.

"Let it bleed a little to wash out any small slivers," Mr. Teach said.

After a few minutes, the blood slowed. They washed the wound and covered it. The whole time they worked, they had heard the loud booms of the *Hannah*'s guns and the answering salvo from the British ship. Suddenly, Hannah realized that it was silent. She peered out a hole in the ship created after a cannonball had crashed through it. At first, she could not see what had happened, but the British ship that attacked them had turned away.

From the top of the main deck of the *Hannah*, she heard a chorus of happy shouts. Then she saw a familiar black shape. The *Sea Serpent* had arrived, its guns blazing, attacking the British ship. The *Hannah* limped back into the fray. The battle lasted for a few more hours, but with two ships attacking it, the British ship was outgunned.

"The British ship is on fire," Daniel shouted as Hannah headed for the rail. A few minutes later, a sailor waved a white flag over the rail of the British ship.

"Stop firing," Mr. Ames called down to the gun crews. But the *Sea Serpent* kept on firing.

"Doesn't Captain Cutter see the flag?" Mr. Ames asked while shaking his head.

The officer holding the flag waved it frantically. But, a minute later, he was gone, struck by a cannonball from the *Sea Serpent.* The *Sea Serpent* fired again and again. Suddenly, there was an explosion that lifted the ship clear out of the water. Three more explosions rocked the ship as it sank. Hannah could see the British sailors desperately trying to free their ship's boats, but Captain Cutter fired once again ensuring no survivors.

Captain Cutter's voice boomed through the speaker horn. "See, I told you that you needed me!"

Dobbs shouted back. "They were waving a white flag."

"Really?" Captain Cutter shouted back. "We certainly didn't see it."

"He had to have seen it. There was no way to miss that poor man out there waving it," Hannah said.

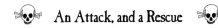

Daniel nodded. “I cannot believe I admired that guy. He is no better than a murderer.”

“We thank you for your help,” Dobbs shouted back to Captain Cutter.

“We will wait to escort you,” Captain Cutter said.

“We are badly damaged. I do not want you to wait as it may be several weeks before we are ready to sail again,” Dobbs shouted.

“Why are you so unwilling to let us sail with you?” Captain Cutter shouted back.

“Why are you so anxious to come with us?” Dobbs said in quick rebuttal.

“You saw how well it worked having two ships. You could sail along, and when a British ship attacks you, we will swoop in and finish them off.”

“You want me to risk my crew to be a decoy for you? No thanks. I know you saw the white flag. You have no honor. You made me ashamed to be an American today,” Dobbs angrily shouted back.

The crew of the *Hannah* cheered at the statement Dobbs had made. Even the lowliest seaman always honored the white flag.

Inside the bay, they saw two large fishing boats. “Ahoy there!” Dobbs shouted. “Is there a shipyard near?”

The fisherman captain shouted back, “Well, I see you are in very bad shape. We heard the guns.” He paused.

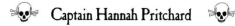

"No British ships are following you into the bay now, are they?"

"The British ship sank," Dobbs shouted back. "My main mast is broken, and my rudder has been damaged. Could you give us a tow?"

Mr. Teach stood behind Hannah and Daniel as the ship was towed across the bay.

"Well, this is turning into quite an adventure," Mr. Teach said. "It makes me think of my great-grandfather."

"Did you see him much?" Daniel asked.

Mr. Teach shook his head. "I saw him once when I was very young. He scared me, I remember. He had a wild woolly beard and hair. People said he tied candles in it to make himself look more ferocious. He was not a nice man, and he came to a not so nice end."

Daniel interrupted. "What do you do on the island at Ocracoke?"

"I am the school teacher," Mr. Teach said. "And doctor when need be. Most of the people in town make their money from salvaging shipwrecks. There are dangerous places where ships run aground or sink. Lately, some people have gotten involved in the slavery business. Nasty work, I think."

Hannah thought of Madeline and nodded. How can people keep others as slaves, she thought to herself.

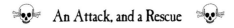

The two fishing boats maneuvered around the *Hannah* and hooks were tightened against the rail. Slowly, the *Hannah* was turned to face the mouth of the bay.

Daniel spoke to Dobbs briefly and then turned to Hannah and said, “Come on.”

“What are you doing?” Hannah asked.

But as she watched Daniel, he turned the capstan to lower the ship’s boat and then she understood. “Oh, good idea, you are going to use the other boats to pull the *Hannah* into the bay.”

Daniel smiled and nodded. Several other sailors began lowering the second boat. Both boats were fastened to the *Hannah*, and they all began to row. With the small armada of boats, the *Hannah* floated into the bay until they came to a large shipyard.

The skeleton of a ship under construction was in the yard, and wooden rails for launching it ran into the water. The ship was a large one, and the unvarnished wood gleamed in the sun like ribs on a giant whale. Men busily hammered and sawed. Hannah saw a small village beside the yard, and she could see the usual collection of saloons, inns, and shops. There was a huge building in the middle of the shipyard and the tracks ran behind it. They could see several other smaller boats—probably fishing vessels—behind the building.

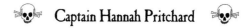

"It looks big enough to handle our repairs," Dobbs said. While Hannah and Daniel waited, Dobbs walked to the huge building and entered a door marked OFFICE. A minute later, he returned with a tall, strong-looking man with bushy eyebrows and a long, pointy nose. He examined the damage.

"It will take at least three weeks, maybe more," the man said.

"I have a very important cargo to deliver," Dobbs explained. "I would appreciate the repairs being done as quickly as possible."

"My name is Aaron Davis," the man said, looking from under his heavy brows. "I am the best shipbuilder in America. You may find someone to do it quicker, but you won't find anyone better."

Dobbs nodded, "Is there an inn nearby?"

"In the village—have your men pack their belongings and tie down whatever you can. We will have to drag her up to the yard," Aaron Davis said.

The next few hours, the crew prepared the ship. The chickens and goats were rowed to shore, and the crew packed their belongings. Hannah tied the cupboards closed. She made sure the fire was completely out in the stove and emptied out the coals. By the time everything was secured, Aaron Davis was ready. A large team of oxen stood waiting to pull the ship out of the water. The tracks were greased and the oxen were attached with heavy chains. Slowly, majestically, the *Hannah* rose from the water to a place near the ship that was under construction. Some of the crew had already wandered off to the village.

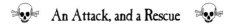

"I would like to go with the others," the man with the burned hand said. His hand was still soaking in the cold water. Mr. Teach took the medicine box and smoothed salve over the burn and wrapped the hand in gauze.

"This will hurt for a while. If it's too bad, try the water again," Mr. Teach said. Thanking him, the seaman ran after the others.

The twins started to follow, but Dobbs grabbed the backs of their shirts.

"Not you two," he said firmly. "You will stay with Jack, Daniel, and me."

"And me, too," Mr. Teach said, huffing to catch up.

Joshua looked disappointed, but Hannah thought that Jonah actually looked relieved that they were not allowed to follow the crew.

"I am sorry, Mr. Teach," Dobbs said. "This is quite an inconvenience for you."

"Quite the contrary," Mr. Teach said. "This is a great adventure. I will have a lot of stories to tell my children." Hannah was about to ask how many children he had when Mr. Teach said, "The goats and the chickens—what will you do with them?"

Dobbs thought for a minute. "I think the chickens will be fine. We will put the crates over there at the edge of the shipyard. Jonah and Joshua can come by each day to care for them. "As for the goats"—he thought for a moment—"perhaps there is a vacant lot in town where we can tether them."

The inn's proprietor must have figured they were a strange bunch, Hannah thought, as they arranged lodging: a paunchy man, a leathered sea captain, twins, and two young seamen escorting three goats. It was called the Wild Rose Inn, and it had painted roses adorning its sign. There was a large common room for the crew, and Dobbs paid extra for two additional smaller rooms. Dobbs, Mr. Teach, and Daniel stayed in one room, and Hannah and the twins in another.

"Is there a place to tie up the goats?" Dobbs asked the proprietor of the inn. The proprietor, a long-nosed, thin woman, hesitated.

"I suppose you could tie them out in the field next to the inn," she said at last.

chapter nine

School

The next few days, they explored the village. There was a small bookstore where Hannah selected two books.

"They must be good," she told Daniel. "Look, it says these are the second printing."

The bookseller, an old man with spectacles, overheard her. "Publishers often do that so that people will think that it's popular." He looked over her selections. "In this case," he said, pointing to a pamphlet titled *Common Sense* by Thomas Paine, "it is a good-selling pamphlet."

Daniel was delighted to find a book about farming. Hannah knew that he still wanted to go back to New York and farm her parents' land that she would have inherited. While she had been at the Red Rooster Inn, she had written a letter to her parents' neighbors asking them to watch over it, and she promised her return someday. But not yet, she told herself. She promised that she would keep fighting until the British were driven from this land.

They went to the beach and let the cold water splash over their toes. The twins built sand castles. Mr. Teach insisted that they spend a few hours a day on their lessons.

"They are bright boys," he said. "Already they are reading, and Joshua is getting very good with his sums."

The next morning, Hannah, Daniel, and the twins set off to continue exploring the village. There was a small assortment of shops, two or three churches, and, at the edge of town, a small brick building with a bell tower on top. She tried to peek through the windows, but Daniel held her back.

"It's a school," he said.

Hannah looked at the twins. She had an idea. A few minutes later, the door opened and children of all ages came out like a stampede headed for playtime. Hannah made up her mind. She went boldly to the door and peeked in at a plump woman seated at her desk looking at some papers. She looked up from her work. Hannah saw, with relief, that although her dress was dark and prim-looking, and her hair was clasped into a tight bun, her face looked very kind.

"May I help you?" she asked. Hannah quickly explained about the ship and how the twins had just started to read.

"We will be here for three or four weeks," Hannah said. "Do you think they could join your class? They are good boys, I assure you."

"Bring them in so I can talk to them," she said, while looking out the windows where the twins waited, sitting on a large rock.

Hannah went out to get them. "They might let you join the school. Be polite and answer the teacher with yes, ma'am or no, ma'am."

Joshua kicked at a loose rock, looking unhappy. "Do we have to?"

Jonah nodded, "It will be fun. Now when people ask us if we have been to school, we can say yes."

Mrs. Hestings, the teacher, talked to the boys for several minutes while Hannah fidgeted nervously outside. At last, she came to the door.

"I would be happy to teach the boys," she said. "They can start tomorrow morning. I will get some of the older boys to bring in some desks for them."

Hannah thanked Mrs. Hestings.

"And how about you?" Mrs. Hestings asked as she turned to go. "Can you read?"

"Oh yes, ma'am," Hannah answered. "I only had the Bible to read back home, but on my ship I have been reading a book of Greek myths that I really enjoy."

"And how about history, science, and geography?" she asked.

"I don't know much about those subjects," Hannah admitted.

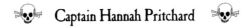

“Then you should join our class. You can study with the older children.”

After Mrs. Hestings had convinced all of them to join her class, they headed back to the inn for the night. Hannah was sure that Mr. Teach would be excited by her efforts toward educating the boys and herself. Hannah still had to check with Dobbs, but she was sure that he would not have any problems with them attending school while the ship was being repaired.

The next morning, bright and early, Hannah, Jonah, and Joshua set off for school. Mrs. Deacon, the proprietor of the inn, had packed each of them a lunch in a small wicker basket. There was fresh bread, cheese, and a cup of water to drink.

“Have a good day,” she said with a cheery wave.

At the school, Mrs. Hestings showed them where to sit. Joshua frowned when he saw they were seated with the younger children. Hannah sat next to a girl about her own age and a slightly younger boy.

“In the city schools, the boys sit on one side of the room and girls on the other. But here I am teaching all eight grades so it is just easier to have each grade sit together,” Mrs. Hestings explained.

The girl leaned over, “I am Lilith,” she said. “And that is Jake.”

"I'm Jack," Hannah replied. She noticed the book that Lilith was studying. "What is that?"

"It's Latin," she said. "We have to pass an exam."

Mrs. Hestings began a geography lesson. Jake and Lilith correctly identified countries around the world, giving brief descriptions of their environments, capitals, and common products. Hannah felt painfully stupid not to be able to name even one. At lunch, she sat with Lilith at a small table outside. Jake sat nearby glowering.

"I don't think that Jake likes me too much," Hannah whispered.

Lilith giggled. "He has a crush on me. He is just jealous."

On the way back to the inn that afternoon, Joshua insisted on stopping at the merchant store to buy marbles.

"Did you know that the Earth is round?" she asked Daniel that night, as they walked along the beach. Daniel scoffed.

"If that were true, all the people on the other side would fall off," he said.

Mr. Teach, who was walking nearby, overheard and explained to them that there is a force of nature, called gravity, which holds everything on.

"Still, if Earth was round and you were on the bottom side you would feel like you were walking upside down," Daniel said reasonably.

Mr. Teach chuckled. "There is no up or down in the sky. So if you are standing on Earth and you are looking to the sky, you are looking up."

Daniel hit his head with his fist. "I don't understand. It's all too much for me. All of this knowledge stuff can really make your head hurt."

Mr. Teach patted his shoulder. "Don't put yourself down. Scientists all over the world are still studying these things and trying to understand them."

Mrs. Hestings also told Hannah about the ancient Egyptians, the Romans, and the Greeks. Hannah was fascinated, and she had reached a point where she didn't feel stupid. She was thirsty to learn more and more as fast as she could.

While Hannah and the twins went to school each day, Dobbs had found Daniel and the crew work at the shipyard to keep them occupied.

Almost every night, Dobbs and Mr. Teach walked from the inn to the shipyard to check the progress of the repairs. One night, Hannah and Daniel accompanied them. When they reached the shipyard, Aaron Davis came out of the office to greet them.

"There were two men here looking at your ship last night," he said. "I watched them from my office window. I thought that they were members of your crew, but they acted suspiciously. They were looking around like they didn't want to be caught."

"What did they look like?" Dobbs asked.

Davis shrugged. "One was tall and dark haired. The other was rougher looking."

"There is an unscrupulous captain named Samuel Cutter," Dobbs said. "We think he has been following us. When we get our cargo, I think he is planning to rob us."

"An American?" Davis asked.

"Sadly, yes," Dobbs answered.

Davis looked disgusted. "As if it isn't bad enough that we have to hide from the cursed British," he said. He looked thoughtful for a moment. "I have an idea. It will be about two more weeks before the repairs are done. Let's wait a few days and then drag the ship behind the building. I think the building is large enough to hide it. I will watch for them to come again, and then I will inform them that you have left already."

"We will have to hide the chicken crates behind the building as well," Daniel added.

"We will need to check at the inn to see if our friends have been snooping around there, too," Dobbs said.

"Hopefully that will work," Davis said. "But you have another problem. The British have a total blockade of the bay. They are not allowing any ships to pass through. If you're caught, the prison ships await."

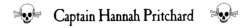

"Perhaps we can sneak out on a foggy night," Dobbs suggested.

Davis looked doubtful.

"What if we hid all the weapons from the hold in the officers' rooms? That way if we did get caught, we could plead the case that we were simply transporting farm goods. Perhaps they would even let us go through?" Dobbs said.

They all agreed that they needed to come up with a creative plan.

The next morning, Dobbs spoke to the men outside of the Wild Rose Inn. "We are moving to the next village. It is about fifteen miles from here."

"What about school?" Jonah blurted out. "Next week we are presenting our projects." He hung his head, embarrassed that he had interrupted.

"You like school that much?" Dobbs asked, surprised.

Jonah nodded, "Mrs. Hestings teaches us all kinds of interesting things, and at recess we play marbles! I've gotten pretty good at it."

Joshua nodded, "Jonah is really good at marbles," he said, generously praising his brother. "He is a lot better than me. He has already won a whole bag of marbles."

Daniel looked at Hannah. He knew that she enjoyed school, too. Perhaps even more than the twins did. Every evening she told him about the ancient civilizations that they were studying.

"Did you know that the Romans had a five-story market?" she had told him the night before. "The bottom floor had shops that sold food. The second floor sold cooking oils and wine. The next floor had spices, and, because they were so expensive, they had hired armed guards. But you will never guess what they sold on the top floor?"

"What?" Daniel asked, looking bored.

"Fish!" Hannah explained. "Water and all—they had a saltwater and a freshwater pond so all the fish were fresh. This was thousands of years ago—isn't that amazing?"

"What do you think you are going to do with all of that knowledge that you are stuffing into your head?" Daniel asked.

"Mrs. Hestings said that people should continue learning for their entire life," Hannah answered.

"What are you going to do when we get to the next village?" Daniel asked.

"I'm going to ask about a school there," Hannah said.

The next day, Dobbs announced that it was time to leave. "I want every trace of us gone for when Captain Cutter comes sneaking around again."

Aaron Davis had already moved the *Hannah* behind the building.

Hannah and the twins went to school one last time to say their good-byes. Mrs. Hestings was almost ready to cry.

"You have all been a delight," she said with tears in her eyes. But suddenly, she brightened. "You could stay with me for the next two weeks!"

Hannah looked at her. "With you?" she asked, overwhelmed by the teacher's kindness.

"I have a small house in the village," she said. "The town council provides it. The three of you would have to sleep on the floor, but I think it will work."

"We could never impose on you like that," Hannah protested.

Mrs. Hestings quickly brushed aside her protests. "The boys can split wood and help me get ready for winter, and you can help me with my cooking and cleaning."

Dobbs had agreed that they could stay there, perhaps relieved that there would be something for the twins to do. He promised to collect them when it was time to go.

"Be careful," he had warned, as the rest of the crew climbed into the ship's boats to row to the next town. They did not need to take the goats because Mr. Teach had found a farmer to take care of them for the next two weeks.

"I don't suppose there is any chance Cutter will come to town, but it's possible. Stay out of sight as much as you can," Dobbs said.

Hannah promised that she would. She watched as they rowed off with Daniel looking a bit forlorn.

"I'll see you soon," she called out after them.

chapter ten

Mrs. Hestings

Mrs. Hestings's home was the tiniest house that Hannah had ever seen. In the kitchen, there was a woodstove and a tiny table with two chairs. There was a small sitting room and a curtained-off space at one side that was her bedroom. Outside, however, a large tree shaded the porch. There was a decent-sized plot for a vegetable garden. A pump near the door brought up cold, clean water.

Mrs. Hestings moved back what little bit of furniture there was in the sitting room and spread several soft quilts on the floor.

"It is probably not wise to mention that you are staying with me," Mrs. Hestings said, as they ate dinner together. "The town council provides the house, and they have a lot of strict rules for the teachers. They may not mind, but I am not sure." Luckily, the house was a short walk from town. "I have taught for so many years that they don't pay much attention to me."

The first day after school, Hannah and the twins set to work on a large pile of wood logs, splitting them and stacking them for winter at one end of the porch. Mrs. Hestings was inside planning lessons for the next day. After a time, she came out and looked at all their work.

"Oh my!" she exclaimed. "I am going to be so spoiled. I have been trying to get my wood split, but most nights I am too tired."

At school, Mrs. Hestings moved the twins into the fourth-year group. The boys were delighted that they no longer had to sit with the youngest children. However, they were dismayed to find out that they had to learn a new kind of writing—cursive.

"She makes us practice and practice," Joshua whined. "Every letter has to be just right. I had to spend an hour making my Os a perfect circle."

"Just be glad that you have the opportunity to learn," Hannah admonished him. "Lilith and Jake are learning Latin—that's another language. But Mrs. Hestings says there isn't enough time to teach me. She says she will stuff me full of science and history, but I feel like a dunce when they have their Latin lesson just the same."

One evening after school, Hannah started cleaning up Mrs. Hestings's garden. She dug up the remaining vegetables and turned the soil over making it smooth for spring. She dug up the potatoes and put them into a basket for winter. Then she decided to go into town to the general store to buy a surprise for the twins for all their hard work splitting wood.

She spent some time in the store trying to select the perfect gifts with the small amount of money she had left. She found a small bag of marbles and a metal beetle toy that lumbered across the table when it was wound up. For Mrs. Hestings, she bought several yards of soft blue wool. Just as she brought her packages up to the counter, she heard a familiar and hated voice.

"I will take some pipe tobacco," Captain Cutter said. "And some of the horehound candy."

Hannah quickly ducked behind a counter, trembling with fright. Dobbs would never forgive her if all of his clever planning went to waste. Cutter must not see her.

While the clerk wrapped up Cutter's purchases, Cutter asked the clerk, "There was a ship getting repaired at the shipyard. Do you know when it left?" Between the stacked display of goods, Hannah could see the clerk shrug.

"The shipyard is a ways from town. I don't pay much attention," the clerk said.

"Did you see any of the sailors in town?"

The clerk hesitated. Hannah held her breath knowing that he had seen her come in the store.

"Sailors don't come 'round here much," the clerk said. "I would ask at the taverns near the wharf." There was a sailor with Cutter. His back was to Hannah, but she felt there was something familiar about him.

"I already tried that. I don't know how we could have missed them," Cutter said after a moment.

"There was a heavy fog three or four days ago. Maybe they left then to sneak past the British ship?"

"I suppose that is what happened," Cutter said, as he went for the door. Just as he reached the door, the armload of purchases slipped out of Hannah's hands. She froze, filled with panic. But the bell over the door tinkled as Cutter and the other sailor exited. She picked up her purchases, breathing a sigh of relief. The clerk gave her a curious stare as she approached the counter. She asked the clerk to fill up two packages of candies.

"Got quite the sweet tooth, I see," he said.

"I am buying them for my friends," she said.

The clerk nodded.

After she had paid and started for the door he asked, "Do you want me to look and make sure that those two are out of sight?" When Hannah paused, he said, "I saw you were hiding from them. I figured they were up to no good. Something about them made me feel uneasy."

Hannah nodded gratefully, and the clerk stepped outside. He looked both ways and said, "I just saw them going into one of the saloons by the wharf."

"Thank you so much," she said, as she quickly ran back to Mrs. Hestings's house.

Her friends were delighted with their presents. Jonah wound the beetle over and over, watching it walk around the floor of the tiny house.

Mrs. Hestings fingered the soft wool. "Oh, Jack, this will make a very lovely dress. Thank you so much."

It was almost dusk, but she still sent Joshua to the shipyard to warn Aaron Davis about Captain Cutter being in town. "Don't let anyone see you," Hannah advised him.

Joshua nodded and set off down the dirt road.

"Why didn't you send me, too?" Jonah said, looking peeved.

Mrs. Hestings knew the story of Captain Cutter and she quickly spoke up, "One boy running down the road is not a thing to notice, but twins are."

Jonah looked embarrassed. "Oh, sorry," he said while nodding.

After a couple of hours, Joshua burst through the door. "Mr. Davis will watch for them so they don't go behind the building. He is going to put the workers back on the new boat so that it looks like they have gone back to their regular work." Joshua's face was red with excitement.

"Did anyone see you?" Hannah asked.

Joshua shook his head. "I was real careful."

"Good lad," Hannah praised him. While Joshua beamed, Jonah glowered. Hannah knew that she would need to give Jonah praise for something.

The next week went quickly. There were no further spottings of Cutter or his men. Hannah was hopeful, and she had allowed herself to relax.

After dinner one evening, Mrs. Hestings hummed a tune that Hannah recognized.

"My mother used to sing that," Hannah said.

Mrs. Hestings saw Hannah's sad face. "Sometimes we try to bury our sorrows when what we need most is to talk about them and to celebrate the lives of those we have lost," she said.

Hannah looked at Mrs. Hestings. Taking a breath, she told her about the day her family had been murdered. "At first I was numb, but now I'm angry." The words continued to tumble out of her mouth as she told Mrs. Hestings about her mother singing and humming around their comfortable house. "She was always cheerful, although she must have longed to go back to the comfortable life that she left in Boston when she had married my father."

She then told Mrs. Hestings of her father: tall and strong and so obviously in love with her mother.

Mrs. Hestings looked at the twins hard at work on the woodpile. "That's enough for tonight, boys," she called out to them.

"At least I have years of good memories," Hannah said. "The twins were too young to remember their parents."

"But now, they have you," Mrs. Hestings said. "And Captain Dobbs, Mr. Teach, and Mr. Grindle. They talk about them all the time. You have all become their family. My students are my family. My husband was a fisherman. One night, his boat capsized in a storm. We didn't have any children, and I grieved for a long time. But then the town council offered me this position. Now I have scores of children. I watch them grow everyday. One day, I will even teach their children. Okay, enough sad talk for now," Mrs. Hestings said. She stood up briskly, "Let's see what we can come up with for dinner."

"Good," Joshua said. "I'm starving!"

The days flew by. At school, Hannah continued to be friendly with Lilith and Jake.

"I wish I could invite you to my house for dinner, but my father would probably send me off to boarding school if I invited a boy to supper." With that, the two embraced in a hug knowing their time was almost up. Jake happened to pass by, and he stopped right in front of them, with his mouth gaping wide open before he snorted and walked off in disgust. They giggled wildly at Jake's jealousy, and Hannah waved farewell as she headed for Mrs. Hestings's house.

"I will miss you so," Mrs. Hestings said that day after school, a few days before Hannah, Jonah, and Joshua had to leave.

"We will miss you, too," Hannah said. "One nice thing about being a sailor is that you make friends all over the world. The bad thing is that you have to leave those friends behind."

A few days later, Hannah and the twins walked along the beach digging for clams. There was a fishing boat tied up, and they watched with interest as the fishermen unloaded their catch. Some of the fish were taken to the local market and the rest were salted for shipment inland.

"Do the British bother you?" Hannah asked one of the fishermen.

The fisherman shrugged. "Not really. We stay in the bay, and the British are more interested in the larger ships anyway."

Hannah counted the days knowing it would not be long before she had to leave. Part of her was excited and anxious to get back on the ship. But another part wanted to stay with Mrs. Hestings. The twins, although fond of Mrs. Hestings, were impatient to be back on their adventure.

On Saturday, Daniel knocked on Mrs. Hestings's door. Mrs. Hestings was helping the twins stack the wood on the porch so Hannah was the first to greet Daniel. "I have missed you," she said simply.

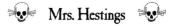

"And I have missed you," Daniel said with a huge grin.

Hannah announced Daniel's arrival to Mrs. Hestings, and she invited Daniel in for breakfast and coffee. He looked around Mrs. Hestings cozy house.

"I should have stayed and gone to school with you." He added with a grin at Hannah, "Although, I am sure you will teach me everything you have learned." He sipped his coffee and told them of the inn that they had stayed at with fleas in the mattresses.

"At night, you could hear mice or rats running around. The food wasn't very good either. I am looking forward to your salt pork and beans."

"When are we going?" Hannah asked.

"Captain Dobbs wants everyone back on the ship this morning. Once I get you and the twins, we will be ready to sail," Daniel said.

Hannah felt a tug at her heart. It seemed as though every time she made friends, she had to leave them. Mrs. Hestings looked equally sad.

"My noisy house will be so empty without you," she said, hugging each of them. "Oh, I almost forgot to give you your present!" Mrs. Hestings ran back into her closet and pulled out a brown paper package. "I remembered that you showed some interest in Benjamin Franklin, and I thought you might enjoy this book. This is a collection of his advice and sayings."

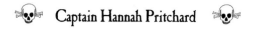

Hannah opened the package and read the title aloud. "*Poor Richard's Almanac*. Thank you very much, Mrs. Hestings. I cannot wait to read this."

She wrapped her arms around Mrs. Hestings. Hannah promised to write her when she could and that she would try to come back and visit someday.

chapter eleven

Inspection

As they made their way to the shipyard, the *Hannah* slid down the launching rails guided by men with ropes. It hit the water with a small splash. The men tied it securely to the deck. They made it all look so easy, Hannah thought.

"She looks beautiful—just as good as new," Hannah said, noticing the gleam it had on its newly repaired body.

"I now believe Aaron Davis. It appears he does do the best work around," Dobbs said as Aaron Davis approached the group. Dobbs showed Davis the letter he had obtained on his trip to Philadelphia from the Continental Congress promising to pay for any repairs. Davis inspected the letter with a frown.

Finally, he handed the letter back. "Well, I suppose if you cannot trust your own government then you can't trust anyone."

"You will receive your payment. I will check back with you. If you have not received payment by the time I have completed my journey, I will personally make it right with you," Dobbs told him.

With that, Davis put his hand out for a shake. It was clear he not only respected Dobbs but trusted him.

"This is all well and good. But tell me, just how do you intend on getting past the British ships?" Davis asked. Dobbs looked thoughtful. "What do you say, Mr. Ames?" he asked the first mate. "Shall we hide our goods or try to slip past them through the fog?"

"Why don't we do both," Mr. Ames said. "Try to slip through the fog, but in case we are not successful, we can hide the cargo as well."

"I have a possible solution for us," Mr. Teach said, joining the conversation. "We will fill up the hold with farm animals. There is a farmer here that is willing to sell me more goats, chickens, and a couple cows. The animals that I cannot use I will be able to sell to my friends and neighbors."

"Oh, that just might work. Thank you, Mr. Teach," Dobbs said.

They spent the next day bringing the cargo from the hold and hiding it among the officers' rooms. Flat crates of guns fit under the beds. Other equipment was spread out and hid throughout the ship. The crates were left behind—not a clue remained of the hidden cargo.

Dobbs saw Mr. Teach coming down the road holding goats by ropes and driving two large cows that were almost ready to give birth.

"Mr. Teach!" Dobbs called anxiously. "Animals that large are going to be difficult to load into the hold."

"We will load them just fine," Mr. Teach said cheerfully. "I told you I was bringing on more livestock. I've still got another load of goats and chickens to add."

Dobbs rubbed his head as if he had gotten a sudden headache. "And just how will we feed them?"

"There is a farmer coming by with hay shortly. Don't worry, Captain Dobbs. I have thought of everything," Mr. Teach said, standing tall with pride. "Now the children on the island will have milk to drink."

When the last of the farm animals were loaded, a hoist was lowered for the cows. Bellowing unhappily, the cows were lifted onto the ship and gently lowered into the hold. The farmer delivered the hay as promised, and it was stacked into the hold.

Dobbs had made arrangements for more wood to be delivered to Mr. Grindle so that he could make several new crates to store corn and oats for the animals. Mr. Grindle also made a couple small fences to close off areas for the cows and goats in one corner of the hold. The fenced-off areas were boarded off in sections for each cow to have her own stall. This kept them safe from getting into the hay that was also stored in the hold.

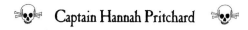

Joshua and Jonah watched Mr. Grindle as he worked, and they eagerly waited a turn to be his assistant. The stalls were made almost directly underneath the door to the hatch. This way, when the hatch door opened, some light would reach into the hold. When Hannah stood at the top of the hatch, she could check on them.

Mr. Teach looked pleased. "That will be perfect. If we can leave the hatch door open, they will be able to get fresh air and light."

"Well, we can leave it open as long as it is not raining," Dobbs cautioned.

Joshua and Jonah patted the cows on their heads.

"If you boys could make sure they have fresh water and hay each day, I think they will be fine," Mr. Teach said. "The Spanish filled their holds with horses when they came to the New World. However, they left them in the dark and did not take good care of them. About halfway across the ocean on their voyage, many of the horses died. There is a spot in the ocean where so many horses were dumped overboard that they call it the horse graveyard and horse latitudes."

Joshua and Jonah's eyes grew big. "That's terrible. Did any of them live?" Joshua asked.

"Yes," Mr. Teach said. "America had no horses. All of the ones that are here now are descendants of ones that were shipped across the Atlantic. There is a herd of wild horses on the Outer Banks that people think survived a Spanish shipwreck by swimming to the shore."

"Wow!" Jonah said. "How do you know so much about everything?"

"From books," Mr. Teach said with a wide smile. "And soon you will be reading books and learning all kinds of new things, too."

"Now, I trust you to take very good care of these cows," Mr. Teach said to the twins.

"We don't have to milk them, too, do we?" Joshua asked, looking nervously at the large animals.

Mr. Teach chuckled. "Don't worry boys. They will not have any milk until after the babies are born."

A thick fog rolled into the bay as they settled the cows in for the evening. Dobbs rubbed his hands together. "Perfect," he exclaimed. "By the time we reach the mouth of the bay, it will be dark. With the heavy fog, we may slip right by."

They bid good-bye to Aaron Davis and set sail through the heavy fog. As they approached the mouth of the bay, Dobbs ordered all of the lanterns to be extinguished.

"Absolutely no talking," Mr. Ames said. "Not even a whisper. Don't move unless you absolutely must."

Although the fog muffled the sounds, Hannah could hear faint noises from the British ship as they left the bay. There was the soft rub of rigging and the gentle flap of a sail from across the water as they slowly turned south. Through the fog, Hannah could see the faint glow of lanterns on the British ship. Slowly, quietly, the *Hannah* sailed past successfully. The lantern glow finally disappeared, and the other ship's sounds could no longer be heard. She allowed herself to breathe normally. They had made it, she thought gleefully.

Suddenly, through the fog and nearly directly in front of them, they could see the lanterns glowing from another unexpected British ship.

"Ahoy!" a voice called. "This is the HMS *Anne*. You are required to let us board and examine your hold. What cargo do you have?" the voice asked.

"Nothing but farm animals and a passenger for Ocracoke," Dobbs said calmly. "We hope to bring back cotton and tobacco."

"I will have to inspect your hold," the voice said. "Stand by to be boarded."

"Go light the lanterns," Dobbs mumbled under his breath. "They will wonder why we went to such pains to sneak past." Several sailors hurried off to do his bidding before the two British officers stepped aboard the *Hannah*.

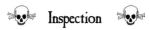

"I am Lieutenant Mark St. James," the first man said looking at Dobbs with a haughty stare. "This is Lieutenant Ramsey. Take us to your hold."

Daniel led the way, holding the lantern for the others. The officers grabbed the lantern. St. James pointed to the stack of crates filled with feed for the animals. He chose a crate near the bottom of the stack.

"Open that one first," he ordered. Dobbs's face was impassive, but Hannah knew that he was seething inside.

"It's just feed for our livestock," Dobbs said evenly.

"We will take a look at it anyway," St. James said sternly.

He motioned for two seamen to uncover the crate and open it. While they worked, St. James eyed the cows.

"Those are fine-looking cows. Where I was raised in England we had cows," he said.

"They are to replenish the herds in Ocracoke that you British stole," Dobbs could not resist saying.

St. James bristled, then he said evenly, "Confiscated, not stole. It takes a lot to feed our troops."

"If somebody takes something of mine, without my permission and without paying for it, I would consider it stolen," Daniel said.

St. James looked down his sharp, pointy nose. "You and your crew are quite feisty." He looked into the box. "Now that one," he said pointing to another crate.

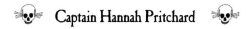

After three more, he seemed satisfied. He climbed up to the main deck. "I'll take a look at the rest of the ship."

Hannah's breath caught in her throat, but she tried to keep her face blank. St. James and the lieutenant looked in the crew's quarters, the woodshop, and the decks. All of these places had some cargo hidden. St. James held up his lantern peering about the main deck, but he was beginning to look bored, as though he had already decided that this ship was not even worth the trouble.

A better search would have uncovered two large crates with weapons right under the ship's boats. But he merely glanced at the boats quickly. Hannah stayed on the main deck as the doors opened to the officers' rooms. Hannah's heart was in her throat, and she was afraid that it would show. Each room only received a perfunctory glance.

St. James eyed the ship's weapons chest. "I ought to confiscate them," he said.

"Please don't," Dobbs said quietly. "There is another privateer we believe is going to attack us and try to steal our ship."

"Real pirates?" St. James raised one eyebrow and shrugged, leaving the weapons alone. "His Majesty's navy would take care of that problem for you under different circumstances." He looked at Dobbs. "I don't understand your objection to being a part of the British Empire."

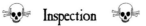

"We want the right to govern ourselves," Dobbs said simply.

"You are all like willful children," St. James said with a disdainful sniff. He stood for a minute without speaking. "We are not supposed to allow any ships to pass. However, I can see that it is going to be a real mess trying to keep all of these animals. It's late, and I'm tired. We are going to let you pass. I don't imagine His Majesty will be hurt for the lack of a couple cows and goats."

With that, he climbed into his waiting ship. Hannah was so relieved that her knees buckled, and she could see Dobbs secretly felt the same way.

Several nights later, Hannah went down into the hold to check if the cows had been given fresh hay. One of the cows acted restless, and she watched for a minute. It made a bawling sound. Hannah held up her lantern, and she could see that the cow had started to give birth. She raced up to the crew's quarters and went straight to Daniel. He was resting in his hammock.

"Daniel! Come quick. The cow is having a baby!" Hannah knew he would want to see it as he had always wanted to be a farmer. She was right. Daniel shot straight up, nearly doing a flip off his hammock.

"I'm on my way," he said, stumbling through the hallway.

"Can we see, too?" the twins said, following Daniel.

"Sure," Hannah said. "But try to be quiet. We do not want to disturb her."

Next, Hannah ran to Mr. Teach's room and knocked on the door. "Mr. Teach? Sorry to bother you, but your cow is having a baby."

"Oh my!" Mr. Teach said. He hurried after her, and the small group watched as the tiny calf fell with a plop onto the straw. Daniel started to step forward, but Hannah took his hand and held him back.

"No, let the mother take care of her," Hannah said. The cow licked and nudged the baby until finally it lurched up on spindly, wobbly legs.

"I've never seen anything like that before," Daniel said.

"Oh, it's so cute!" Jonah said, holding his hand over his mouth.

"It's amazing that they can stand and walk around so quickly right after being born!" Joshua said.

"I suppose that way they would have a chance to escape from predators," Mr. Teach guessed. "I need to get my herd on the island before it gets any bigger," he said with a chuckle.

The journey continued and there was no sign of British ships or the *Sea Serpent*.

After two weeks of sailing, they approached the island. "It is very dangerous around Ocracoke. The sand goes far out and creates sandbars. Many ships have wrecked here.

People sometimes call it the graveyard of the Atlantic. In low tide, there is sometimes only five feet of water. I would recommend anchoring a ways out and bringing the cargo in by using the ship's boats," Mr. Teach said.

Dobbs looked worried. "How are we going to get those cows onto the shore?"

"We will just hoist them into the largest of the ship's boats," Mr. Teach said with a smile.

Dobbs rubbed his head as if another headache had hit him, but he nodded in agreement. "We will unload the cargo first," Dobbs said.

Mr. Grindle had made new crates for the guns and animal feed. They packed the hidden bundles into the new crates and sealed them shut. These were also loaded onto the ship's boats, and seamen took turns rowing them to shore. Hannah took her turn rowing to shore with the goats and chickens.

"I've got a good place to hide those supplies," Mr. Teach suggested. He then led them to an old ramshackle barn, where they could cover the crates of weapons with straw until the patriots could come across the sound and retrieve them.

"I will have a man row to the mainland to contact the leader of the colonial militia about retrieving the supplies," Dobbs said. They walked back to where they had left the ship's boat.

"Shall I come help you load up the cows?" Mr. Teach shouted out to Dobbs, who was still on the ship.

"No, you stay there, but Jack you come back," Dobbs replied.

Hannah and several other seamen rode the largest of the ship's boats and tied it up securely.

Dobbs looked at Hannah and pointed, "You will carry the calf. The rest of you can help me with the mother cow, and the other cow will be loaded during the next trip. The mother may be more willing to come if they see Jack taking away the calf."

Hannah picked up the calf, who struggled to get away from her. She was surprisingly strong, and it took all of Hannah's strength to hang on to her and climb out of the hold with her. Once again, the cow was hoisted over the edge of the ship, bellowing and protesting the entire time. They gently lowered the mother cow into the boat that Hannah and the calf were in, and the boat rocked precariously while she gained her footing. Hannah was concerned that she would capsize them. The mother cow, however, seemed at ease as soon as she caught sight of her calf. Several sailors climbed into the ship's boat and rowed them to shore.

Hannah tied rope around the cow's neck, and Mr. Teach tried to coax her to step off the boat onto land, but the cow stubbornly refused to move. Hannah grabbed the calf and stepped into the sandy water, taking the calf to the shore. The calf mooed pitifully for her mother. This time, when Mr. Teach pulled on the rope, the mother cow stepped out, waded through the water, and ponderously treaded onto the shore to get next to her baby.

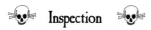

"Now, we have to get the other one out of the ship, and we don't have a baby to entice her," Mr. Teach said a little worried.

They rowed back to the ship, and the crew lowered the second cow into the boat. As they started for land, Hannah thought how lucky they were that everything had gone so smoothly. Then, suddenly, about halfway to shore, the boat lurched as it bumped into a sandbar. The cow lurched and scrambled trying to keep her footing. But she toppled over against the side of the boat tipping Hannah and the other sailors into the water. Hannah came up spluttering. Luckily, the water was warm and not too deep. She could see the cow swimming instinctively for shore, as she and the sailors tipped the boat right side up.

After realizing that everyone was safe, the men on shore hooted loudly with laughter. "It's about time you took a bath!" they yelled.

Hannah stepped onto the shore and wrung out her wet clothes.

Daniel and a couple of the other sailors trailed behind in the smaller of the ship's boats with the nanny goats and some of the chickens. The rest would be left on the ship for meals as they continued their voyage.

Ocracoke was a tiny town of winding streets and small cottages. It was slightly swampy, allowing trees to grow, making it shady and cool.

"You must come to my house for dinner," Mr. Teach said. "My wife will never believe all of my adventures unless you confirm them."

Leaving the rest of the crew back to explore the tiny town, Hannah, Daniel, the twins, and Dobbs followed Mr. Teach to his house. As they walked through the streets, people ran out of their houses with welcoming waves.

"Henry, you are back! We were worried about you," several people said.

They stopped at a small house with a barn and pasture. A man with bushy red hair and a mess of freckles came to the gate.

"I have something for you, Fred," Mr. Teach said, as he delivered the cows.

Fred was so happy he appeared ready to cry. "These are wonderful animals. Now we will have milk, butter, and cheese in town again." He took the ropes and led the cows to the pasture. "I will pay you for these as soon as I can," Fred said.

"I know you will, but don't worry about it," Mr. Teach said with a smile.

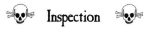

Mr. Teach's cottage was small but neat, and a wooden fence surrounded the yard. A vegetable garden was on one side, and there was a small barn in the back. A billy goat stood beside the barn in a small fenced area that kept him out of the vegetables. Mr. Teach led the three nanny goats from the ship into the fenced area, and the twins followed carrying the crates of chickens.

"I bet those chickens will be glad to get out of there." Mr. Teach chuckled, as Jonah and Joshua set them free in their own pen.

"Did the British miss that goat you have there?" Daniel asked.

Mr. Teach shook his head. "It was the strangest thing. About a year ago, he just wandered into town. No one knew where he came from."

Hannah looked at Daniel. "Mr. Tibbs?" She said breathlessly.

"No one found a fat orange cat, did they?" Hannah asked.

"Not that I know of," Mr. Teach said.

The full impact of discovering the goat struck Hannah. If that really was Mr. Tibbs, then the treasure could not be far away. They had left Mr. Tibbs, the goat, and George, the ship's cat from the *Sea Hawk*, behind when the British had captured them. Dobbs looked at her with a raised eyebrow but made no comment.

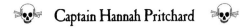

The door opened and a horde of children of all different ages tumbled out of the house. At first, Hannah thought that the children might be his school pupils, but they all cried, “Papa, Papa!” and ran to hug Mr. Teach. A woman followed, carrying a small child. She handed the baby to one of the older children and smothered Mr. Teach in a long embrace.

“Oh, Henry,” she sighed, kissing his whiskery cheek. “I have missed you so much.” She was taller than Henry and nearly twice as wide, but it was obvious that she loved her funny little husband. Her warm brown eyes danced with pleasure. She hugged Hannah, Daniel, and Dobbs in turn as they were introduced.

“Thank you so much for returning my husband,” she said, wiping happy tears from her eyes.

The children, too, seemed to adore their father. They clambered around him eager to hear about his trip. Several of the children were sent to the dock with a wagon to retrieve Henry’s trunk of school supplies.

“You must stay for supper,” Mrs. Teach said, even before Mr. Teach had told her that he had already invited them. “The children dug up clams last night. I was going to just cook them, but if the goats can be milked, we could have a good clam chowder.”

“I can help,” Hannah offered. “I’m the ship’s cook.”

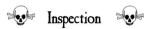

"Tonight you are a guest," Mrs. Teach said firmly. "As you see, I have plenty of helpers."

"How do you manage?" Hannah asked.

"Well, we have an easy system. Each child helps take care for the next youngest, that way I only have to watch the youngest two or three." She handed Hannah the baby. "You can hold him if you like while I cook."

Hannah held the child gingerly. She had never been around a baby before. "Don't be afraid of him. He won't break," Mrs. Teach said, taking out a pot nearly as big as the ones Hannah used in the galley. The baby yawned and looked up at her with sleepy eyes. Mrs. Teach told her to put the baby in a basket on the floor. "No brothers or sisters?" she asked Hannah.

Hannah shook her head, "one bro . . ."— she hesitated— "sister, the British and Indians killed her and my parents."

Mrs. Teach stopped working and gave Hannah a hug and said, "You poor dear." She brushed Hannah's cheek. "The wind is drying out your skin. I have a lotion that will help you."

"It doesn't matter," Hannah said, brushing at her cheek. Hannah wondered if Mrs. Teach suspected she was a girl.

In the dining room, there were two long plank tables. The smaller children ate first to free up chairs for guests.

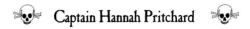

Mrs. Teach ladled steaming bowls of clam chowder and passed a platter stacked high with biscuits.

"By the way," she said as they ate, "there were two men here looking for you a few days ago."

"For me?" Mr. Teach asked.

"They were asking about Captain Dobbs's ship, and they told me that you were a passenger."

Dobbs put down his spoon with a worried expression. "Did they tell you their names?"

"There was a very tall fellow named Samuel Cutter. He said he was captain of the *Sea Serpent* and a friend of yours. He claimed that he had saved you from a British attack."

Dobbs nodded. "And the other man?"

"A very rough character," she said. "Mean little eyes—said his name was Larson."

Hannah looked at Dobbs and gasped. "Do you think it's the same one?" Then it hit her. "That is why the man in the store with Captain Cutter seemed so familiar and that explains why Cutter knew about the treasure."

"Larson was a sailor, who sailed with us on the *Sea Hawk*. He stole some of the captain's Spanish doubloons and hid a couple in Jack's belongings to cast the blame on him," Daniel said.

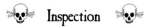

"I was almost lashed," Hannah shuddered with the bad memory. "Then Dobbs and Daniel found where Larson had hid the rest of the coins."

"We dropped him off at an island, and he somehow became part of Cutter's crew. That's why Cutter is so convinced there is a treasure. Larson told him. He might have thought the treasure went down with the *Sea Hawk*. But then Thomas said that we were looking for treasure, and he put two and two together," Daniel said.

"Larson told me a story about the stolen doubloons, but he told it another way," Mrs. Teach said. "He claimed that he was the one wrongfully accused. He was either trying to earn my sympathy so I would tell him anything that I knew, or he simply likes to hear himself talk that much. Even as he was telling me, I knew it was a lie. And now that I have met you, I am sure of it. Captain Cutter seemed polite enough, but there was something about him that made me nervous. I think he could cut your throat without blinking an eye. He said to tell you that he was heading to the islands to load rum and sugarcane."

Dobbs snorted, "He knows very well I don't want to join him. I wonder what trick he has up his sleeve now."

After the chowder dishes were cleared, and the tables were wiped, Henry took out his violin. Then several of the children ran to their bedrooms. They returned with various instruments, including violins, flutes, drums, and wooden spoons that made a clicking noise when they were played against a leg. The Teach family gave a concert. They sang several rounds of songs for their guests in high, sweet voices.

At last, Dobbs stood up. "This has been so nice. I hate to leave, but we do need to get back to the ship." With warm good-byes and the promise of a visit again, they headed out for the ship.

It was near dusk, and Hannah shivered, wondering if Cutter had really gone to the islands, or if he was somewhere nearby watching them.

"If that goat was Mr. Tibbs, the treasure cannot be far away," Daniel remarked.

Dobbs nodded. "In the morning, we will take one of the ship's boats and go down the coast. Hopefully, the wreckage of the *Sea Hawk*'s boat is still there. Although, after two years, it maybe gone."

"We might recognize the cove. There was a swamp there, I remember," Daniel said.

"With any luck, we will be on our way home before Captain Cutter even knows we're gone," Dobbs said.

chapter twelve

Treasure

Early the next morning, as soon as breakfast had been served, Dobbs ordered the largest of the ship's boats to be lowered into the water. It was a fine, warm day that fed Hannah's optimistic mood. Daniel looked excited, too. They armed themselves well, with swords, pistols, and knives. They brought three men from the crew in addition to Daniel, Hannah, and Dobbs. They were Ivan, John, and Floyd. "Just in case," Dobbs had said. Mr. Ames would sail the *Hannah* with the rest of the crew south. They would keep the ship's boat in sight as they worked their way along the shore, looking for the location of the buried treasure.

Hannah was exuberant. "Maybe we are going to find it and maybe George, too."

Dobbs shook his head. "We don't know that the goat was Mr. Tibbs," he said. "One goat looks pretty much like another, and George, if he did survive, would be wild by now. Once a cat goes feral, you cannot tame it."

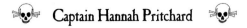

In spite of Dobbs's words, Hannah felt hopeful. George had been the ship's cat, but he had also been a constant companion for Hannah. She had managed to save George and Mr. Tibbs, but she had been forced to leave the animals behind when the British captured them.

They came to what appeared to be a promising cove, and Daniel climbed out for a look. He was back in a few minutes shaking his head. Hannah hopped out at the next cove. She only had to take a few steps to know that it was not the right place.

"No trees or swamps," she reported while getting back into the boat.

By the time they had checked the sixth spot to no avail, Hannah was getting discouraged.

"We will find it," Daniel said with an encouraging pat on her arm. They rowed around a slight curve in the island. Hannah saw it first: an orange cat sitting on top of the wreckage of a small boat.

"George," Hannah called, not sure if she was happier to see the cat or to find the treasure. By the time they managed to maneuver the boat through the rocks, George had disappeared. Then Hannah saw him sitting near a small shady patch of trees.

"George," she called out to the cat again. Even from there, she could see that the cat had a hard time surviving. His coat was tangled with burrs, and he was frightfully thin. She took a few steps forward, but, each time she did, the cat ran farther away. Finally, she sat down in a patch of tall grass with her back turned to the cat.

The men were looking for the grave, which seemed to have disappeared. When they had buried the treasure, they used a wooden cross to mark the treasure, but it made the spot look like a grave. There was no sign of the wooden cross, however. Dobbs pointed to a spot, and the men started digging.

Hannah could hear George quietly sneaking up behind her. She stretched out her hand. A minute later, George carefully sniffed her fingers. Then she heard the familiar purr. George leaped into her lap, and she stroked him gently.

"It was lined up with those three trees," she heard Daniel say. "It's got to be here." He took the shovel and poked it into the sand at several spots. The last thrust made a loud thunk.

"I think I found it!" Daniel shouted with glee.

Dobbs told Ivan and Floyd to dig, but, just as they did, six men stepped out of the woods. One man held the point of his sword at Daniel's neck. Hannah could see another man, Larson, pointing his sword at Dobbs.

Captain Cutter strode into the clearing next. "Nice of you to save us all the work of finding the treasure," he said. He pointed his sword at Ivan and Floyd. "Dig quickly," he commanded.

Another sailor from Cutter's crew held John at sword point. John's eyes met Hannah's, but he quickly looked away, so as not to reveal her hiding place. The men from the *Sea Serpent* had not noticed Hannah. They had their backs to her, and she was hidden by the sea grass.

Hannah knew that she had to take action. Cutter and his men would not hesitate to kill her shipmates. She was the only one who could save them. She slowly pulled out her pistol. She wanted to shoot Larson, but she could not get a clear shot without risking Dobbs.

She aimed at the man threatening Daniel and fired. The man screamed, and a bright splotch of red appeared on his chest as he slumped to the ground. There was immediate chaos. In the same instant, Daniel and Dobbs drew their swords. Hannah stood up and pulled out her sword from its scabbard. She rushed into the fight. Counting Cutter, there were seven men from the *Sea Serpent*. However, with the man Hannah had shot down, the sides were now even.

Hannah leaped and jumped back skillfully avoiding the slashing swords. There was the loud clang of metal on metal as they fought. The sword was heavy. Hannah held on to it with both hands. She fought standing back-to-back with Daniel, and they protected each other. One of the men from the *Sea Serpent* struck her sword, almost knocking it out of her hand. The sailor's next thrust sliced her arm and blood soaked her shirt. She leaped aside.

"Stand still you little monkey," the man growled.

"No, you stand still!" Hannah shouted as she ran her sword through him.

Hannah looked for Larson and saw him as he knocked Dobbs's sword from his hand. Before Dobbs could pick it up, Larson made another thrust and plunged the sword into Dobbs's chest. Larson pulled his sword back up and raised it over his head to finish Dobbs, but he rolled out of the way just in time.

"No!" Hannah screamed.

Charging fearlessly at Larson, she swung her sword with every ounce of her strength. The blow hit Larson's neck and nearly severed his head. He looked surprised, and then fell in a bloody heap beside Dobbs.

Hannah's intervention had bought Dobbs enough time to get his pistol out. He aimed it at the man fighting with Daniel and fired. The man fell to the ground instantly. Hannah looked around. The battle was almost over. Now there was only one man from the *Sea Serpent* still fighting. Daniel and John quickly engaged him and killed him. Captain Cutter was nowhere to be found.

She heard a groan behind her. Whirling around, she saw that Dobbs had slumped over, holding a wound on his chest. Hannah tore off part of her vest and tried to stop the bleeding.

"Captain Dobbs," she sobbed. "You can't die. We'll get you back to the ship. Leave the treasure," Hannah shouted. "Daniel help me get Dobbs into the boat."

"No," Dobbs muttered. "Don't let this all be in vain. I am in pain, but it's not too bad. Just hclp mc on thc boat," Dobbs said. Leaning heavily on Hannah, Dobbs climbed into the ship's boat.

Hannah looked frantically at Daniel. "Let's go quickly. Bring the treasure."

Floyd and Ivan had both been killed. "Put their bodies on the boat, too. They deserve a proper burial at sea," Hannah said to John and Daniel. After they loaded the bodies, they carried the treasure chest to the boat as well.

"Where is Captain Cutter?" Hannah cried out.

"He must have slipped away while we were fighting—the coward," Daniel said.

Hannah saw George out of the corner of her eye. She ran over and scooped him up. "Hurry!" she shouted as they started rowing. "I'll bet Cutter is going back to his ship."

They reached the ship and fastened the chains to the boat. When they reached the deck, several men carried Dobbs to the captain's quarters and laid him on the bed.

Hannah undid his shirt and tore several strips of a sheet in a continued attempt to stop the bleeding.

"Go and call the crew," Dobbs said weakly, as he struggled to sit up. "I've got to guide my ship."

Hannah pushed him back down. "I can do it," she said firmly. Dobbs looked at her and then to Mr. Ames, who stood in the doorway.

"Do as Jack says," Dobbs told Mr. Ames.

Mr. Ames hesitated for a second, but nodded and said, "Yes, sir."

"I will leave the sailing in your capable hands Mr. Ames," Hannah said quickly. "But take us into deep water where the *Sea Serpent* can't drive us aground." She looked at Daniel. "Can you read charts well enough to get us to Portsmouth?"

"I think so," Daniel said as he nodded, grateful for his lessons with Dobbs.

"I can help Daniel as well," Mr. Ames said stoutly. Hannah was happy to see that Mr. Ames no longer looked angry that Dobbs had not chosen him to lead the fight. Mr. Ames disappeared from the door. A minute later, Hannah heard the capstan pulling up the anchor. Hannah washed and inspected Dobbs's wound. A small cut on his back showed where the sword had gone all the way through his body. The twins fetched the medicine box. When they returned, their eyes were wide with fear.

"Is Captain Dobbs gonna make it?" they asked together.

Hannah shook her head. "He is hurt pretty bad. Bring me some grog."

The twins scampered away to obey her orders, and Hannah hurried back to the captain's quarters, where she washed the wound with a strong soap. The twins came back with the grog, and Dobbs drank it down quickly. Hannah threaded the needle. She motioned for the twins to hold him, but Dobbs shook his head.

"I might holler and moan, but I won't move." Hannah tried not to show her fear. What would they do without Dobbs, she thought. He couldn't die, he just couldn't. She held up the needle, took a deep breath, and set to work.

"I didn't know when I taught you how to sew wounds that one day you would be sewing up my own," Dobbs said through gritted teeth.

Hannah smiled at him. "I never imagined I would be sewing you up either," she said, while concentrating on one of the last stitches. She had closed Mr. Dobb's chest wound and bandaged him with more torn strips of sheet.

"Thank you," Dobbs said, his voice so low that Hannah had to bend close to hear him.

"You were a good patient," she said trying to sound cheerful. Although the outside of the wound was closed, she wondered how much damage had been done on the inside. Dobbs seemed to be having problems breathing.

"Sleep," she ordered him. "I'll go sew up John and come back to check on you." Dobbs nodded and closed his eyes. She tiptoed out and closed the door.

John was not as good a patient as Dobbs. He yelped at each pinch of the needle. The cut was a nasty slash all the way down to the bone in his arm. It took many stitches to close. She had to have two seamen hold him so she could finish the job.

After she was done, she peeked in on Dobbs. "I'm all right," he said waving her away feebly. In spite of his protests, Hannah noticed that he looked pale, and beads of sweat gathered on his forehead.

"Try to sleep again," she said, hoping to sound more optimistic than she felt.

On her way to the galley, she saw Daniel. "You have been so busy tending to everyone else. What about the cut on your arm?" he asked. Daniel rolled up her sleeve to inspect the gash further. It was a long cut but, fortunately, not too deep.

"Sit down," he said. "I will go get some gauze from the medicine chest."

"I am fine," she said.

"I said sit down," Daniel said firmly. "We are going to fix that arm."

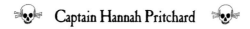

“Yes, sir,” Hannah responded in mock obedience. Daniel disappeared and returned with fresh gauze and a clean rag to wash out the wound.

He wrapped it tightly, gave her a pat on the shoulder, and said, “Now you can go.” She flashed him a smile and walked to the galley.

She started cooking the evening meal. Nothing fancy tonight, she thought—just salt pork and beans. She had finished soaking the pork and putting it on boil when Daniel came in to the galley.

“I just climbed up and looked through the spyglass,” he said. “I saw a faint black speck. It looks like the *Sea Serpent*.”

chapter thirteen

The Plan

"I have a plan," Hannah said. They sat at the table while she told Daniel the details of her idea. "What do you think?"

Daniel nodded. "I wonder what Captain Dobbs would think?"

"I'm going to check on him. You get the men gathered on the main deck."

Dobbs was still sleeping, but he awoke when Hannah came in. "The *Sea Serpent* is following us, but I have an idea," Hannah said. Quickly, she told Dobbs her plan.

"That just might work," he said weakly.

"I will tell the others," Hannah said.

She gave him a worried look, but she could not think of anything else that she could do for him. As she left the room, she saw Jonah. "Get your brother and sit with Dobbs. If he needs water or tea, get it for him. If he starts moaning or thrashing about, come get me."

Jonah nodded and ran off to get his brother. By now, Daniel had all the men gathered on the main deck.

"The *Sea Serpent* is following us. She is a faster ship. I have no doubt that she will catch us," Daniel explained.

"Why don't we just give them the treasure?" one of the men asked.

"Captain Cutter leaves no survivors. He has attacked his own country's ship so he has even more incentive to not leave any survivors. By attacking us, he has crossed a line from privateer to pirate. He could be hanged," Mr. Ames explained.

"I have a plan," Hannah said. "We don't want them to catch up to us at night. We'll try to outrun them, but I don't think we can. However, I don't think they will catch up until tomorrow, so we have all night to prepare. Now, he won't want to sink the ship, at least until he has the treasure. I think they will fire grapeshot at us and then board us. When the ship gets close enough, we'll all go down into the hatches. When they fire the grapeshot, I want you all to pretend like you've been hit. They have about the same number of crew. We killed six on the island so we might have more. We'll let a lot of them board. Then we will jump out from hiding places. We have six pistols, so with any luck, we can take out a few before the fighting starts. Do not show yourselves until I give you the signal.

I am hoping Captain Cutter will be so anxious for the treasure that he will board quickly as well."

Mr. Grindle stepped forward. "Before they board the ship, they will climb up and look at our deck. If they don't see bodies, they may be more careful."

"I had thought of that," Hannah said. "Could you make some forms that are roughly man shaped? We can put clothes on them and lay them around the deck. We will have Dobbs's bloody shirt to use on them to make it look even more realistic."

"And mine," John shouted.

"I think we should also lay out the bodies of Ivan and Floyd so that is the first thing they see when they board the ship. That way, they may not look as closely at the fake bodies," Mr. Ames said.

Just as he spoke, Joshua came running to Hannah. "Captain Dobbs wants everyone to come to the captain's quarters."

Hannah led the way up to the quarterdeck. Dobbs struggled to sit up, and Jonah tried to help by propping up pillows behind him.

He gave Hannah a weak smile. "Gather 'round." He coughed and tiny drops of blood flew out. "Daniel and I named this ship the *Hannah*," he said to the assembled crew, "because she is the bravest and strongest girl that we know. She was with us on the prison ships, and she fought side by side with us to capture this ship. She saved my life, and I would fight next to her and trust her as much as any one of you. So fight hard and don't let Cutter take my ship after all our efforts. I have listened to Hannah's plan and it is a good one."

"Hannah?" several of the men said. "Who is Hannah?" Dobbs turned to Hannah. "May I tell them?" he whispered soft enough so that no one else could hear.

Hannah hesitated. As Jack, she would have the men's respect. Would they feel that way about a girl? After a long moment of contemplation, she nodded.

"I told you all the story about the *Hannah* because the real Hannah is a trusted member of our crew." There was a moment of stunned silence.

Finally one voice said, "Jack?" Everyone turned and stared at Hannah.

"That's why you never grow any whiskers," one man said with a chuckle.

"Will you follow her directions for the fight?" Dobbs asked.

The men all looked at one another, some of them nodding and others frowning.

"I know it will take some getting used to," Hannah said. "But I am still the same person I was five minutes ago. You can still call me Jack if that makes you more comfortable."

After most of the men had nodded in agreement—some reluctantly—they filed out talking quietly among themselves.

"Stay," Dobbs said to Hannah and Daniel. "I am dying."

"No," Hannah sobbed. "Don't say that."

"It's true. I've been having trouble breathing, and it's getting worse. I wanted to be sure things were settled here before I died. Take care of each other. You have been like a son and daughter to me. I love you both."

Dobbs closed his eyes. After a few more minutes, Dobbs let out a shuddery breath, and he was gone.

"We love you, too," Hannah cried. Daniel hugged her, and she sobbed into his shoulder. Tears streamed down his face as well. After a while, she wiped her eyes on his shirt. "I'd better go tell Mr. Ames," she said.

"I will go check on how much closer the *Sea Serpent* has gotten," Daniel said, as he left to climb the mast with the looking glass. The crew members spent the rest of the night rearranging the deck to make hiding spots.

"Where did you put the treasure?" Hannah asked when Daniel returned.

"In the back of the chicken crates where the goats were," Daniel answered.

"And George?" Hannah said suddenly. "Where is he?"

"I put him in your room," Daniel said.

Hannah went to her room. George sat on her bed. He jumped up and meowed. She took a brush and started to work on his fur. She brushed out some of the burrs, and, after a while, she went back up to the galley. Battle or not, the men had to eat. By evening, they could see the *Sea Serpent*. It was still far enough away that Hannah did not think it could catch them before morning. Mr. Grindle had finished five forms. They were dressed, and they looked real except that they had no heads. The crew laid them on the deck so that the tops of the forms were hidden.

"Hannah, did you see the bodies we made with Mr. Grindle?" the twins asked excitedly, as they came on deck. Hannah had not told them about Dobbs's death, and she couldn't bring herself to tell them when they seemed so happy.

"I did. I'm sure Mr. Grindle couldn't have done it without you," Hannah said, patting Jonah on the back as she spoke. The twins scampered off to brag to the other men about their work.

Hannah slept restlessly that night. George curled up beside her, purring. At first light, Daniel knocked on the door. "They are really close," he cried out.

Hannah scrambled up. Over the rail, she could see the *Sea Serpent* bearing straight for them. Two or three hours until they reach us, she surmised—just enough time to feed the men. She quickly made porridge and had the twins deliver it with an apple for each man.

"You boys are not to go on deck until I tell you," Hannah instructed them both.

Joshua groaned, but she thought that Jonah looked relieved.

"Pass out the weapons," she told Daniel.

"You two men bring Ivan and Floyd's bodies and leave them in plain sight on the deck," Hannah said.

The *Sea Serpent* had been following directly behind them. Now, however, she had maneuvered as if she were going to pass them. As the men gently laid the two seamen's bodies on the deck, Hannah looked around to make sure that the stage was set. There needs to be more blood, she thought. She quickly took two of the chickens from their crate. With her knife, she cut off their heads. As the headless bodies jerked about, blood splattered across the deck. She held them by their feet allowing the rest of the blood to pool on the deck.

"Get below!" she told everyone.

Daniel brought in the weapon's chest, and Mr. Ames passed out pistols, swords, and knives to the crew.

"Stay below until we're sure they are done firing," Mr. Ames reminded the crew. "Then come carefully on deck and get to your spot."

"Don't forget—scream loudly," Hannah added, as everyone crowded down the hatches.

"What if they do not fire grapeshot?" one of the men asked.

"They will," Hannah said. "Grapeshot is designed to kill people but not to damage ships."

They did not have long to wait. A few minutes after the last man climbed down the hatches, a large boom came from the *Sea Serpent* and a thunderous rain of shrapnel, nails, chains, and pieces of metal tumbled onto the deck. The men opened the hatches a tiny crack, screaming and moaning loudly, "I'm hit! Help me!"

After several minutes, Captain Cutter yelled over, "Ahoy there, *Hannah*! Surrender the treasure, and we will let you go. You have my word." Except for a few men crying out with pretend injuries, the deck was silent.

"Take your places," Hannah said softly. The men climbed out of the hatches. Keeping low, they tucked themselves into hiding spots on the deck. They waited in intense silence while Captain Cutter called out to them several more times.

"Maybe we should hang out a white flag. Captain Cutter doesn't honor them, but he will think that we do," Daniel said. Staying low, Hannah rushed to the captain's quarters. She tore a large strip from the same sheet she had used for bandages. Racing back down, she flung it over a section of rail that had not been damaged by the grapeshot. There was a soft bump and a rope ladder was attached with hooks. Hannah hid under a tarp covering the remaining chicken cages. She saw two sailors climb nimbly through a stretch of broken rail.

"Looks like they are all dead or wounded," one of them shouted back. Hannah willed the men to hold their attack until Captain Cutter stepped onto the deck.

At last, Cutter stepped onto the *Hannah*. "Find that treasure chest!" he commanded. "Look in the captain's quarters first."

"Now!" Hannah screamed. An earsplitting roar of gunfire exploded on the main deck from the men armed with pistols. She fired her own pistol at Captain Cutter, but the bullet only grazed his arm. Some of the other men had done better. Several of the *Sea Serpent*'s crew lay mortally wounded, and the *Hannah*'s crew had already engaged the others with swords and knives.

Cutter had drawn his sword and was headed toward Daniel. More men were coming on to the *Hannah* from the *Sea Serpent.* Hannah looked for Cutter and saw him fighting Daniel. Hannah ran to help. Cutter came down hard on Daniel's sword, and it flew out of his hand. With an evil grin, Cutter thrust it again, but Daniel cleverly jumped out of the way.

"You could have been a great hero," Daniel said. "You could have been remembered in history."

Captain Cutter laughed. "I would rather be rich."

He stabbed at Daniel, who again evaded him but was now backed up against the bullwark. Cutter grinned again and raised his sword dramatically. He was so intent on Daniel that he had not seen Hannah sneak behind him. She raised her sword and stabbed deep into Cutter's back. Cutter's sword clattered to the floor. He turned slowly.

"Killed by a cook?" he said incredulously.

"No, killed by a woman, Hannah Pritchard," Daniel said. He thrust his sword into Cutter to finish him off.

"Get him off of our ship!" Hannah cried. Together, she and Daniel lifted his body and tossed it over the rail into the ocean. There was a splash as he hit the water.

"Let the sharks have him," Hannah said.

They hurried back into the fight, but it was nearly over. One by one, Cutter's crew was pitched into the ocean. The men all set up a cheer when they saw Hannah return. Only two of their crew had been killed, but several had injuries.

"What shall we do with the *Sea Serpent*?" one of the men asked.

Hannah hesitated. "We should board her and see if there is anything to be salvaged. But it is an evil ship. We should destroy it."

They cautiously boarded the ship, wary of a similar trap. But the entire crew had boarded the *Hannah*, except for the cook and the cabin boy, who remained hidden below in the galley.

"Please," the cook pleaded. "I didn't know what kind of man Captain Cutter was. I just joined the crew this voyage, and the cabin boy is only eleven years old."

Hannah looked at him, and she knew he was telling the truth. The cabin boy was white with fear.

"I could use some help in the galley," she said after a moment. "Get your things and come with us."

In the captain's quarters, they found a large chest. Hannah gasped when she opened it. The chest was filled with unspeakable treasures. Gold and silver coins, pearls, ruby necklaces, gems, and gold bracelets piled nearly to the top of the chest.

"I wonder who they stole these from. This must be worth much more than the chest of doubloons," Daniel said, stunned at the size of the treasure.

Hannah looked at Daniel and grinned. "There are going to be some mighty rich sailors if we can get this back to Portsmouth."

They stripped the ship. Before they left, Hannah and Daniel started several fires. Then they went back to the *Hannah* and unlatched the hooks, letting the *Sea Serpent* drift free.

It was almost nightfall. This was the time when the *Sea Serpent* would have been in all its dark and evil glory. But now the flames crawled up the black sails and across the deck. The crew stood on the deck of the *Hannah* and watched as the *Sea Serpent* drifted farther and farther away. At last, the fires reached the gunpowder hold and caused a great explosion. With a mighty roar, the ship vanished beneath the sea.

"Well, Hannah, you certainly came up with a good plan," Daniel said.

"No, that was a great plan," Mr. Ames added.

chapter fourteen

New Beginnings

Later that evening, Hannah went to her room. Now that the battle had ended, she finally had time to grieve for her friend. "What are we going to do without him?" she said to George as she gently stroked his furry back. She lay down onto her bed, sobbing into her pillow until at last she fell into an exhausted sleep.

When she woke, she could see from the light that it was late morning, and the men were way overdue for their breakfast. She hurried to the galley feeling ashamed that she had not upheld her duties. Seamen were already hard at work cleaning up the bloodstains and dismantling the fake people. When she entered the galley, she saw Mr. Pimm, the cook from the *Sea Serpent*, wiping down the table with a rag. Joshua, Jonah, and Tim, the cabin boy from the *Sea Serpent*, were scrubbing the pots and pans and putting them away.

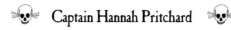

"We saved you some," Mr. Pimm said, setting a bowl of porridge in front of her. "Don't worry. The entire crew has been fed."

"Thank you," Hannah said. "I have never slept that late before."

"Mr. Ames told me about your friend Captain Dobbs. I am sorry to hear about his death."

Hannah ate her breakfast quickly and went to find Mr. Ames to discuss the sea burials. He was busy supervising the sewing of the sailcloths to make shrouds for the bodies of the crew that they had lost. Daniel gave her a worried look as she approached, but she smiled, letting him know that she was fine.

"I thought we should make the shroud for Captain Dobbs ourselves," Daniel said.

Hannah ran to Dobbs's quarters and selected Dobbs's favorite shirt—the one he usually wore on Sundays or on special occasions. His bloody shirt had been used to set the stage for the *Sea Serpent.* Lovingly, Hannah dressed him and combed his hair. Daniel had followed her in with sailcloth and needles. Swallowing back the lump deep in her throat, Hannah and Daniel began to sew. Mr. Ames brought a cannonball to weigh the body down. When they were done, they carried his body out together and laid it on the deck. The other slain seamen were already entombed in their shrouds.

"Would you like me to do it?" Mr. Ames said. Hannah nodded, and Mr. Ames took out a Bible and read several passages. He then asked for a moment of silence. One by one, the bodies were tossed into the sea until only Dobbs remained.

Hannah stood in front of the men. "Captain Dobbs was a wonderful friend and a great captain. I hope that we can all follow his example of integrity, bravery, and kindness."

Almost reverently, Mr. Ames, Daniel, and Hannah lifted Dobbs's body over the rail and dropped him into the sea that he had loved his entire life.

Hannah climbed the ropes halfway so that she could see the spot where Dobbs disappeared under the waves. The men remained gathered on the main deck. Hannah turned to look at them while still clinging to the ropes.

"While everyone is here we should take a vote for our new captain," Hannah said.

Mr. Ames stepped forward. "We actually did that this morning while you were sleeping."

Hannah tried to hide her irritation. "Don't I get a vote?" she said.

Mr. Ames shook his head, "Some thought that because I was the first mate, I should be the captain. But this ship doesn't belong to me. I was not the one who planned our victorious battle. I did not ensure that we are sailing home

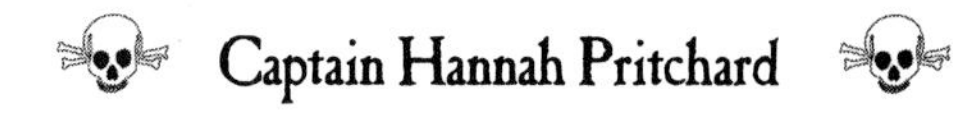

safely to our families with that amazing treasure. The men voted and it was unanimous."

"Who?" Hannah asked.

Suddenly, the crew started laughing and cheering all at once. "Hooray for Captain Hannah! Hooray for Captain Hannah!"

"I will be proud to serve you as first mate," Mr. Ames said with a smile.

"And I will be your navigator," Daniel said.

Hannah stepped down from the ropes overcome with emotion. She fought back tears, but she knew that this was not the time to act like a girl. George wound around her feet, purring loudly. Hannah bent down and picked him up.

"All right, men," she said, smiling from ear to ear. "Let's set out for Portsmouth to divide up this buried treasure!"

the end

The Real History Behind the Story

Although Hannah Pritchard is a fictional character, her adventures in this story take place during an important turning point in the American Revolution.

Winning America's Independence

After several delays, the French fleet finally arrived in the United States in August 1781. The French fleet had 29 ships and 3,200 men. The British immediately engaged them in a battle known as the Battle of Chesapeake. Historians are divided on who actually won the battle, but it did weaken the British resolve and allowed the French to block General Charles Cornwallis from receiving reinforcements. The French admiral sent empty transport ships to Newport, Rhode Island, to transport some French troops to Virginia.

George Washington was determined to take back New York City, but the British were firmly entrenched there, especially on Manhattan Island. Washington's troops were outnumbered. Jean-Baptiste Donatien de Vimeur, comte de Rochambeau met with Washington and convinced him that a better opportunity presented itself in Virginia.

Jean-Baptiste Donatien de Vimeur, comte de Rochambeau was commander of the French forces in the United States during the American Revolution.

Washington pulled a very clever hoax on General Henry Clinton in New York City. He set up heavy artillery around the city and dug trenches as though he was preparing for a battle. But behind the trenches, he moved out his entire army on a seven-hundred-mile march down to Virginia. For once, Washington, with the addition of the French troops, outnumbered the British. Cornwallis surrendered after they surrounded Yorktown, Virginia, in a wide semicircle around the entrenchments, putting the British under siege on September 28, 1781. Finally, on October 19, 1781, Corwallis's army marched out of Yorktown in surrender, virtually ending the war.

Prison Ships

Even though the war had ended, it took the British nearly a year to vacate New York. During all that time, they left the prisoners of war on their prison ships. Historians estimate that eleven thousand to thirteen thousand men and women died of starvation and disease aboard these ships.

British general Charles Cornwallis (right, with sword) surrenders to General George Washington and his officers at Yorktown.

Benjamin Franklin traveled to France during the American Revolution to gain French support. The support of the French army and navy was crucial in the American victory over Great Britain.

Benjamin Franklin

Benjamin Franklin was a printer by trade. He was also a wise and witty man, known for such sayings as "Early to bed, early to rise, makes a man healthy, wealthy, and wise." He gathered these sayings in a book called *Poor Richard's Almanac*. He was also an inventor, inventing such things as the Franklin stove, bifocals, and the lightning rod to protect houses during storms. While he was the first postmaster of the United States, he invented the odometer to help him map out routes. Franklin made two trips to France before the war began to ask for loans for the government, which he received. After the war began, he made one more trip to France in December 1776 asking for help, which resulted in the French navy and Rochambeau's troops coming to America.

Blackbeard the Pirate

Blackbeard was a notorious pirate who terrorized the Carolina coast and the West Indies, sinking ships and taking prisoners for ransom. Blackbeard's real name was either Edward Teach or Edward Thatch. He was known for his ferocious appearance. He wore a long red coat with a bandolier with knives and pistols, and he carried two swords at his sides. It was rumored that

Edward Teach, better known as Blackbeard, made his name terrorizing the Carolina coast and the West Indies. His name became forever linked to piracy, and his legend grew immensely through the years.

he displayed cannon fuses in his wild hair to increase his devilish appearance. The Royal Navy finally captured Blackbeard near Ocracoke in 1718.

Many people believe that Blackbeard had named Ocracoke, but it is actually from the Wocco Indian tribe's original name, Wokokon.

The Lighthouse

The sea around the Outer Banks near Ocracoke, North Carolina, is full of shifting sands known as the Diamond Shoals. At low tide, the water can be as shallow as five feet. Even at high tide, it is often only twelve feet, and sandbars exist in unexpected places. Hundreds of ships sank in these waters, and the people of Ocracoke made a living from scavenging these wrecks. To warn ships away from the shoals, lighthouses were built. The first Cape Hatteras lighthouse entered operation in 1803. The current lighthouse was built in 1868, and it was first operated in 1871.

Pistols

Most fighting in the late 1700s was still done with swords. Although pistols were in use, they were very inaccurate, except at close range. They also had to be reloaded with powder and ball and tamped down with a tool attached to the gun, making it impossible to fire rapidly.

Further Reading

Fiction

Klass, Sheila Solomon. *Soldier's Secret: The Story of Deborah Sampson*. New York: Henry Holt, 2009.

Penn, Audrey. *Mystery at Blackbeard's Cove*. Terre Haute, Ind.: Tanglewood Press, 2007.

Torrey, Michele. *Voyage of Plunder*. New York: Alfred A. Knopf, 2005.

Nonfiction

Fradin, Dennis Brindell. *The Battle of Yorktown*. New York: Marshall Cavendish Benchmark, 2008.

Lewis, J. Patrick. *Blackbeard, The Pirate King: Several Yarns Detailing the Legends, Myths, and Real-Life Adventures of History's Most Notorious Seaman*. Washington, D.C.: National Geographic Society, 2006.

O'Donnell, Liam. *The Pirate Code: Life of a Pirate*. Mankato, Minn.: Capstone Press, 2007.

Internet Addresses

American Revolution.org: France in the Revolution

<http://www.americanrevolution.org/frcon.html>

**National Geographic Kids: Blackbeard—
Pirate Terror at Sea**

<http://www.nationalgeographic.com/pirates/bbeard.html>

PBS: Liberty! The American Revolution

<http://www.pbs.org/ktca/liberty/>

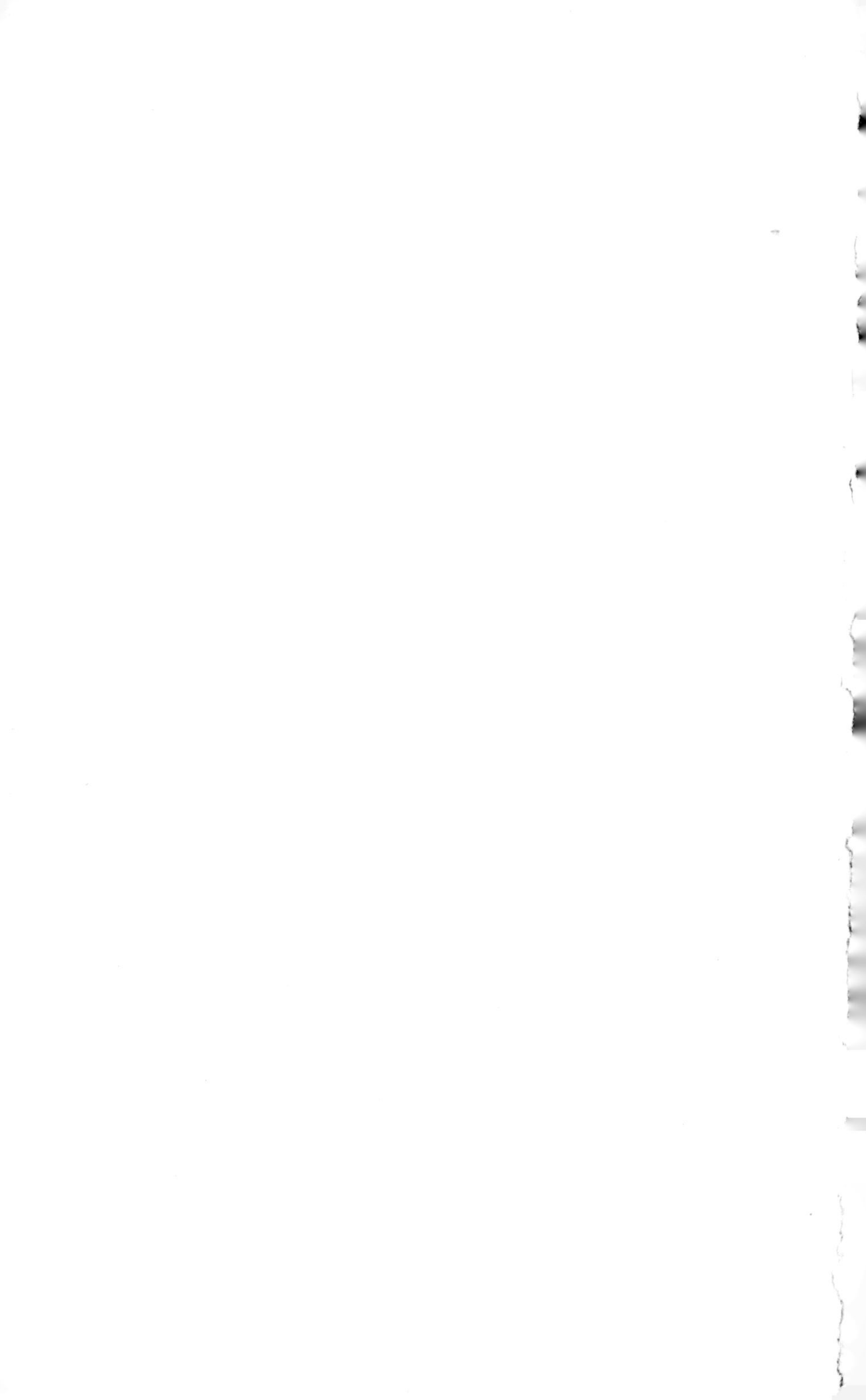